The Unexpected

JENNIFER RENOT

outskirtspress
DENVER, COLORADO

This is a work of fiction. The events and characters described herein are imaginary and are not intended to refer to specific places or living persons. The opinions expressed in this manuscript are solely the opinions of the author and do not represent the opinions or thoughts of the publisher. The author has represented and warranted full ownership and/or legal right to publish all the materials in this book.

The Unexpected

v2.0

Outskirts Press, Inc.
http://www.outskirtspress.com

ISBN: 978-1-4787-0429-4

Outskirts Press and the "OP" logo are trademarks belonging to Outskirts Press, Inc.

PRINTED IN THE UNITED STATES OF AMERICA

Chapter 1

Mike came home and was really tired and not really in the mood to get into another fight with Sarah. He went up the stairs and found her asleep in bed. That was a first that she wasn't waiting up for him to give him the third degree on not coming home for dinner and not calling her. He got undressed and climbed into bed. He rolled over and put his arm around Sarah and fell asleep. When he woke up the next morning he didn't see Sarah in bed with him so he got up and took a quick shower. He put on his jeans and went downstairs and saw Sarah making some eggs and bacon. She smiled at him when he came down the stairs not wearing a shirt.

"That smells wonderful. How long have you been up?"

"Not long I figured since you probably haven't eaten since I made you breakfast yesterday I would make you a big breakfast for you. So was there a break in the case?"

Mike wasn't sure why she was even remotely concerned about the case even though it had consumed a lot of his time lately. The look on his face must have had a confused look on it because Sarah smiled at him and laughed.

"Don't act so surprised that I'm asking about the case. I

don't want to know details I just want to know when I'm going to get my husband back that's all."

"I see that's what you were really after. You don't care about the case just want to know when I'm going to be home more often again."

"I don't want to fight with you Mike not today. I'm trying to work on our marriage and it's really hard when you aren't here. I love you Mike but sometimes I don't feel like you love me as much as you love your job."

"Sarah I told you that things were going to change when I took this position with the FBI. I'm not just a cop anymore I have to get more in depth and more involved in the cases I take and peoples live depend on my decisions I make. I thought you understood that when I took the job."

"I did back then but it's like I live with a stranger. I don't know how you feel anymore and we haven't had any us time since you got the job. I would like to have kids some day before I get too old to have any. You do want to have a family don't you?"

"Yes of course I do. Just right now is not a good time. We finally got the case solved and I can finally take a vacation. Why don't we work on this marriage away from here? Let's go on a vacation and have our alone time and maybe we can work on that family you want so bad."

Mike gave her a little wink and she smiled again. She put the eggs in front of him and sat down. She was still smiling when they were done eating and she had cleaned up the kitchen. Mike had gone on the computer to see where they could go and found a little romantic getaway. She was now looking over his shoulder and saw what he was looking at and she had a glow about her. He smiled and they talked about where they were going to go and when they were leaving. When they had made all the arrangements Mike called his office and told him that he was not to be disturbed and was going out of town for a week or so. When it was confirmed Mike and Sarah started packing. Mike was going to drive to give them more time to talk and spend more time together. When their bags were packed and they were ready to go they packed up the SUV and they headed out of town. Sarah was so excited and for the first time in a long time Mike realized how much he had missed being with Sarah. He loved her smile and her long brunette hair and how her face lit up when she smiled. Sarah was in charge of the map and the directions while Mike drove them to the destination. They had been driving for quite a while before they both were getting hungry again and they decided to get something to eat. They saw a mom and pop restaurant off the side of the rode and they decided to go in. They were seated and looked over the menu and decided on burgers and fries and when the waitress left Sarah was looking at Mike.

"What?"

"Are you sure you are okay with this? I mean I know it's going to be hard not being included in work stuff and not having anything to do."

"Sarah I wouldn't have done this if I didn't think I could handle it besides this place brings back memories of the mom and pop diner we first met."

"Oh yeah the cop with his partner and the klutzy waitress that was a moment to remember."

They both started laughing but the memories from

when they first met came back to Mike and he really had missed Sarah a lot. Since he got the job with the FBI he was home less and all they seemed to do was fight and it made him not want to come home sometimes but he did almost every night. There were a few cases that he stayed in a hotel because he couldn't sleep and needed to keep working. That case had kept him on his toes and awake for almost a week straight but then it was finally over. The last case had taken over a month to finally break and seeing how happy Sarah was made him realize that he had been gone an awful lot and that wasn't fair to her. The fights were of frustration and he knew that she was only concerned about him and he had shut her out all that time instead of letting her in. When he got the FBI position he had completely shut Sarah out and now he wished he hadn't done that. He was glad that she hadn't left him and wanted to work things out between the two of them and the thought of having a little one of them put a smile on his face. He must not have realized that it was a really big smile until Sarah looked at him a little puzzled.

"What are you thinking about?"

"I was thinking of a little one of us running around."

"Are you serious about that? I mean I know that your job means a lot to you and I don't want to get in the way of what you love to do."

"Sarah I have put my job before you for so long that right now I want to work on us and put you first. I don't know why you stayed with me for so long."

"I meant what I said when we said our vows Mike. It was for better or for worse and this was just a worse time for me but I didn't want you to miss out on the opportunity for the

FBI position because I saw the look on your face when you got offered the job. I wasn't going to be the one that told you that you couldn't do it. I wanted to stand by you and I have for the most part. I guess when you got the job and you shut me out I was mad at you but in a way I wasn't fair to you. I always had to pick a fight with you and I guess that was my way of getting you to talk to me and get your attention. I went about it all the wrong way and I apologize for that."

"Don't apologize I was an idiot to put my job before you in the first place. I mean yes I love my job but I shouldn't have let it consume me and I shouldn't have shut you out. I guess I shut you out because I didn't want you to know what I was going through and I thought the less you knew the less harm you would ever be in. Some of the cases I took could have been really bad if I got too close and they went for you because of me and I couldn't live with myself if anything would have happened to you. I figured the best way to keep you from harm was to shut you out of my life. I went about everything the wrong way too. I guess this little vacation will help us both out and work on things we both should have done from the start. I guess I just thought helping other people was what I was meant to do but then I think back and it hurt my marriage instead."

"I don't blame you for wanting to help other people Mike that's just who you are and you are wonderful at what you do. I don't want you to think that you have to stop helping people to be with me."

"I know but I should know my limits and what you need and want should have always come first."

"Well let's put all that behind us. We are going to work

on us now and that's what really matters. You want to change and so do I. That's why we are on this vacation to get back what we lost and find ourselves again."

"I think I can handle that. I want us to be how we were when we were first married. We had some really great times then."

"It's only been five years since we got married so it shouldn't be too hard to get back there."

Sarah smiled at Mike and they ate their food and started to discuss the next few hours of driving. Mike decided that it would be a good idea to get some gas while they were stopped and then head back out again. They finally got to the small town they were staying and found the lodge where they were going to be spending the rest of the week. It was a little cottage that was out in the middle of nowhere surrounded by woods. It had a nice fireplace and a big kitchen and there were two bedrooms. The master bedroom had a Jacuzzi in the bathroom and the bathroom was really big. The other bedroom was smaller but had an adjoining bathroom much smaller than the master bedroom. In the back there was a hot tub surrounded by woods. They were really going to enjoy this place. The first thing they did was unpack and got in the hot tub. They relaxed for a while and then went back in and Mike started to make something for them to eat. They enjoyed a candlelit dinner and then went to the bedroom. Mike didn't waste anytime on working on making a family.

They had been there for a few days and finally Sarah insisted that they go shopping. Mike didn't really want to go but went anyway. He was parking the SUV after he dropped

Sarah off to do some shopping and was going to meet her somewhere for lunch. She kissed him goodbye and they agreed to meet at one of the restaurants at the end of the strip. Mike sat at a table by the window waiting for Sarah and when she saw him she crossed the street. Mike waved to her and saw her crossing the street and the look of terror in her eyes before he heard gunshots and two cars plow into his wife. He shot out of his seat and went to his wife who lay lifeless in his arms. She had been shot several times and all the things she had purchased were scattered all over the street. The two cars had been on a shooting binge and he called out to have someone call the police. The police were there and had gotten her to the hospital. Mike was pacing the hospital floor when the doctor came over to him.

"Mr. Stratford?"

"Yes how is my wife?"

"I'm sorry we couldn't save her. She was barely alive when she got here but she lost so much blood and there wasn't anything we could do. I'm sorry."

Mike didn't know what to do. He was so mad he wanted to punch the doctor but knew that wasn't going to bring Sarah back. He sat down and put his head down in his hands. The doctor left and told him that he could see his wife one last time before they put her in the morgue. Mike said his goodbyes to his wife and had tears falling from his eyes as he left the room. He was passing the waiting room when a couple of the cops stopped him.

"Mr. Stratford we are very sorry about your wife. I know this probably isn't a good time but we need to ask you some questions."

Mike agreed and told them what he saw and then they left him. He wasn't sure what he was going to do now. He kept beating himself up because he should have been with her and would have been able to get her out of harms way but he wasn't. They were finally working things out and he should have been there to protect his wife. That's what his job was all about protecting people but he had failed at that with his own wife. He didn't know what he was going to do now.

Chapter 2

Mike went back to work and had a hard time focusing on the case in front of him. He couldn't think of anything except the last look he saw on his wife's face before she was shot and plowed down by two idiots. He hadn't slept well since then and he had his coffee when there was a knock on the door. He looked up and saw his boss there.

"Agent Stratford I think you need to take more time off. You aren't focused and we need you to be focused."

"I can't and I probably never will. I think I should just leave and give you my notice now."

"I wouldn't go that far. It's only been a couple months since your wife's death and I'm sure that it is really hard for you to get over someone you love. I understand that but quitting isn't the answer. You just need to take more time off and get your head on straight."

"No I think it would be in everyone's best interest if I just leave. I don't want to be the cause of anyone else dying because of a stupid mistake. I just don't have what it takes anymore."

"Well if you should change your mind the door is always open."

"Thanks. I have never lost anyone close to me before and I guess it's really hard to deal with this."

"Take all the time you need."

His boss left and he stood up and took his wife's pictures and other personal items out of the office and went home. When he got home it was so gloomy and he didn't feel like being there at all. It was only torture seeing Sarah's things and pictures hanging up and he needed to get out of there. He went to the bar and had a few to drink.

"I knew I would find you here."

"Sam what are you doing here?"

"Mike this is not the way to cope with this."

"This is how I deal."

"Well maybe you should come over to my house. Tony and I would like to see you again."

"Sam it hurts to much for me to deal with this. I loved Sarah like you wouldn't believe. I know we had our problems but we were working on our marriage. I should have been with her when she wanted to go shopping instead I dropped her off and told her to meet me at a restaurant for lunch. I shouldn't have done that. If I had been with her it wouldn't have happened I would have been able to protect her."

"You don't know that. Quit beating yourself up so much. Listen let me take you home you don't need to be drinking anyway that's what dad used to do."

"I quit my job today so maybe I'll turn out to be just like dad."

"All right it's time to go. As long as I'm alive you aren't going to turn into dad. Let's go."

Mike put his drink down and followed his sister out of

the bar. He got in her car and they headed to her house. He got out and sat on the couch and Sam got dinner ready. Tony came home shortly after Sam got dinner started.

"I guess you finally found him?"

"Yeah he was at the bar again. He's been going there a lot lately and I know that he is depressed but I worry about him. He told me that he quit his job today and I know that there is really something wrong. He loved his job and helping people."

"Losing Sarah must have done something to him. I guess you haven't told him yet?"

"No how am I supposed to tell him I'm pregnant when he was working on a family of his own with Sarah before she was killed?"

"I don't know but he's going to find out one way or another."

"That is very true."

Sarah finished dinner while Tony got changed and they all sat at the table. Mike picked at his food and he tried to look like he was okay but he wasn't doing a very good job. Sam and Tony both tried to make conversation with him but Mike was non responsive. Finally Sam let it out.

"Tony and I are having a baby."

Mike looked at her and tried to smile but Sam knew that he was happy for them but it was hard for him to say or do anything with the information.

"Mike you need to snap out of this. You can't live your whole life in a shell and not get on with your life. That's what Sarah would have wanted you to do. She wouldn't want you moping around for the rest of your life and afraid to get close to anyone again. I am not asking you to find another wife I'm just saying don't shut me out too. I love you Mike but I am not going to sit around and watch you lose touch with reality."

"I'm doing the best that I can all right. I've been trying to deal with this for so long that I don't even know what to do with my life. I keep blaming myself for her death and yet at the same time I don't know how to live without her."

"You will move past this just like we got past mom's death."

"That's not the same. Mom was never there for us and neither was dad. Sarah and I were working on our marriage and a family and now I'm not ever going to be able to be a father or a husband. I am really happy for you both but I can't take this anymore. I want to go home."

"Why so you can mope around with Sarah's pictures and drink yourself to sleep?"

"No I need to pack up her things it's been a few months and I guess that's the only way to start working on getting passed this."

"It's a start but I think that you should just sleep here tonight and then tomorrow since I have the day off I will go over and help you out."

"I don't need you babying me Sam all right. Just take me home or I'm going to walk there myself."

"I'm not babying you Mike I'm trying to help you."

"Well stop I don't need your help."

Mike got up from the table and slammed the door shut behind him. Sam was going to go after him but Tony grabbed her arm.

"Don't go after him he needs time to himself."

"That's what I'm afraid of Tony. When he goes off by himself he doesn't think. I don't want him to do anything stupid."

"You need to give him space. You haven't given him any space since the funeral. You've been over there every night and check up on him every day. He needs his space."

"I can't help it he was always there for me growing up and I just want him to know that he's not alone anymore and that I'm here for him."

"He knows and I'm sure he appreciates what you are trying to do but he needs to cope with this on his own."

"I guess your right. I'll leave him alone for a while."

Tony smiled at her and she sat back down. They finished their meals and went to bed.

It had been almost a year since Sarah's death and Mike still hadn't gone back to work. He had finally gotten all of Sarah's things boxed up and put in the attic. He started to spend more time with Tony and Sam again. When Sam had her baby girl, Ashley, Mike came around a little bit more. He was an uncle and he wanted to be in Ashley's life. He was babysitting her when Sam and Tony came home.

"How was the movie?"

"It was okay if you like love stories."

Sam hit Tony and he pretended that it hurt. Mike laughed a little bit and was going to head out.

"Why don't you try dating again Mike?"

"Sam I'm not ready right now. I don't think I'll be able to ever find another woman to love as much as Sarah."

"You don't have to fall head over heels for a woman you just met."

"I think I need more time for that."

"Well I guess I'll have to tell Monica that you aren't going to date her then."

"Sam what did you do?"

"Monica works with me and she sees your picture on my desk a lot and always asks how you are doing and everything so I thought maybe she should ask herself. She is too chicken to ask you out so I said that I would set you both up. It's just a date you don't have to marry her."

"Sam why do you do this to me?"

"I want to see you happy again."

"I am happy being alone and spending time with Ashley. I'll go out with her this one time but don't ever do this to me again."

"Are you serious?"

"Yes but it's the only time. You try to hook me up again and I'm not ever going to speak to you again."

"All right thanks Mike you won't regret this."

Mike rolled his eyes and left. He couldn't believe that his sister was trying to set him up. What was this world coming to? Mike went home and went to bed.

Mike picked up Monica at seven and they were going to eat and then see a late movie. She got in the car and they headed to the restaurant. He opened the door for her and was a perfect gentleman but Monica could feel that this was awkward. When they had ordered and were waiting for their appetizers she finally spoke.

"I'm sorry if you didn't want to go out with me."

"It's not you Monica. I just haven't been on a date since Sarah and I'm a little out of practice. I'm sorry."

"You are doing great in my book. How are you doing anyway?"

"Better. Since Ashley was born it's been easier for me to get Sarah out of my head a little bit better but I still miss her."

"I don't blame you. If you don't want to go to the movie I would understand. I don't want to seem pushy or anything."

"Monica can I ask you a question?"

"Sure."

"Why did you agree to go on a date with me anyway?"

"This is awkward but here goes. I saw a picture of you on Sam's desk and I've wanted to actually date you since then but you were with Sarah and I guess I was hoping that we would hit it off well enough tonight that you would want to see me again. I guess that's not going to happen though is it?"

"I don't know. I mean you are an attractive woman but I don't think my heart is even ready for a relationship right now. I think I need more time but I don't want you to think that it's because of anything you said or did."

"I told Sam it was too soon but she was the one that insisted that you needed to get out there again."

"You got to love my sister."

They both laughed and talked a little bit more and Mike decided to see the movie and then dropped her off at her house. She thanked him for the good night and told him that she was around if he just wanted a friend. He thanked her and headed home. He did think Monica was an attractive woman but he wasn't quite ready for that kind of commitment yet. He was glad that Monica understood and didn't have to break her heart. He was going to have words with Sam tomorrow. When he got up the sun was shining through his bedroom window and he finally decided to get up. The phone was ringing when he got out of the shower. He answered it.

"Hello?"

"So how did it go?"

"No more setting me up. She's attractive but there isn't anything between us."

"Are you going to turn every woman down?"

"For now yes. I'm not ready yet Sam. I'm doing the best I can to not mope around anymore but it's still hard to get out of bed. I just don't think I could handle it if I fall in love again and something else happens."

"You always think so negatively Mike."

"Well I can't help it. I still keep seeing the look of terror in Sarah's eyes before she was gun down and hit by the cars. I can't help it if I don't want to have to ever go through any of that again."

"So what are you going to do miss out on love again because you feel guilty?"

"Yes. If I don't fall in love then I can't hurt anyone and no one can hurt me. Listen I have things I want to do so I'm going to let you go."

"You don't have anything to do you just want to drop the subject. I'm not done with you Mike. You will fall in love again I can guarantee that."

"I wouldn't bet on it. You will lose and I'm done with this conversation now."

Mike hung up and got dressed. Sam was right he didn't really have anything to do but he didn't want to talk to her anymore about his feelings. He had gotten better since Ashley was born. The day Sarah was buried he vowed that he was never going to fall in love again and he planned on sticking to it. He didn't want to have to worry about making the wrong mistake again and putting someone else's life in danger. That's why he had quit working with the FBI. He didn't work and was doing just fine. He did have a hobby now though and that was remodeling the house. He decided to get started on the kitchen. He figured if he remodeled the house then it wouldn't remind him so much of Sarah. He had redone the whole upstairs and now was working on the main floor. He had started on the kitchen first and was in the middle of making new cabinets. If he kept himself busy he didn't think of Sarah. He usually only thought about her when he went to bed or when their song came on the radio but that was it now. He wasn't sure what he was going to do when the house was done being remodeled. He didn't want to think about it right now and just work on the kitchen and go from there.

Chapter 3

Mike had just finished the kitchen remodeling and was going to take a shower when the phone rang.

"Hello?"

"Hey Mike how are you doing?"

"Fine how are you Sam?"

"Good. I was calling to check up on you I haven't seen you for the last few days."

"I just finished remodeling the kitchen. I was actually going to take a shower."

"Well I don't suppose tomorrow you would mind watching Ashley for a while would you?"

"Sure I don't mind where are you and Tony going?"

"Tony has an awards ceremony for his accomplishments at the company and he wants me to be there but it's a grown up thing and we can't bring Ashley with us. I mean if you had plans or something we could find someone else."

"No don't do that I would love to watch Ashley."

"Thanks Mike. You're the best brother ever."

"I'm your only brother."

"I don't care you are still the best."

"I'll see you tomorrow then."

Mike hung up and smiled. He took his shower and then got some take out food and watched television for a while and then went to bed. He woke up and the sun wasn't up yet it was still early. That was a first for him. He usually wasn't awake before the sun and slept for as long as he could. He decided to get up and take a shower then got dressed. He was looking at the kitchen and what a great job he had done and decided to make himself something to eat for breakfast. He had to be at Sam's in a couple of hours so that Tony and Sam could drive to the place they were having the awards and then were going to drive back later that night. Mike was planning on staying the night over there just in case they decided to stay the night if it was too late. He packed a small bag and then headed over to Sam's. When he got there Ashley was crying and Sam was trying to calm her down and was panicking on what she was going to wear. It was complete chaos and Mike took Ashley from Sam and comforted her. Ashley seemed to like Mike a lot and would stop crying when he held her. She was still a few months old but she still liked it when Mike was around. Sam and Tony got their things together and headed out. They got in the car and headed to the hotel where the ceremony was being held. They were going to get changed there so that they didn't wrinkle their clothes and since it wasn't until seven they still had plenty of time before then. They had to get there early to do a rehearsal for some of the ceremony and Sam was nervous but she wasn't sure why she wasn't the one getting the awards.

"Sam calm down."

"I'm sorry I don't know why I'm so nervous you are the one getting the awards not me. I hope that everyone likes me."

"They will love you Sam. I'm just glad that Monica could cover for you tonight so that you could be with me. I really appreciate you being there for me."

"Tony I love that you are getting recognized for all the hard work you put into that place and I love you."

"I love you too. I just can't believe that this is happening."

"Well you better believe it. I'm proud of you for everything that you do."

"Well thank you that means a lot to me. I know lately I've kind of been somewhere else but I finally got the job done I needed to get that account and now I got the company even more money."

"I think they should give you a raise or something."

"Well awards are nice too."

"They don't pay the bills and don't keep Ashley satisfied."

"She's still young wait until she starts to walk and talk then we are going to have start pulling money out of nowhere."

They started laughing and when they got there they had the valet take their car. They walked in and were showed where the rooms were to change and put their things in the hotel room and then wandered around to check out the place. They saw the ballroom where they were going to be having the ceremony and there were two huge chandeliers hanging from the ceiling and there were people setting up the room. Tony saw his boss and walked over to him with Sam right by his side.

"Hey Tom this is my wife Samantha."

"Samantha it's great to finally meet you. Tony talks about you all the time and I'm glad you could make it."

"Thanks Tom. You can call me Sam that's what every one else calls me."

Tom nodded and started to talk to Tony. They went over what was going to happen and then he had to tend to some other things and said he would see them later. He had mentioned that after the ceremony that there would be dancing.

"Do you want to stick around for the dancing?"

"We can stay for as long as you want Tony this is your night. I'm just here for moral support."

"All right but if you get bored we'll leave."

Sam smiled at him and then they decided it was time to get ready. Sam called and checked on Mike and Ashley and Mike assured her that everything was fine. She finally hung up and got ready. Tony was wearing his tuxedo and Sam had gotten a long black dress; which showed off her curves and put in the diamond earrings that Tony had gotten her for their five-year anniversary two years ago. She put on her makeup and wore her hair partly down. She was putting on her shoes when Tony whistled at her. She blushed and smiled at him.

"You look amazing Sam."

"Thanks you don't look so bad yourself."

"Are you ready to go meet the rest of the crazy people I work with?"

"I guess I'm as ready as I'll ever be. Show me the way."

Sam took Tony's arm and they went down to the ballroom. There were a lot of people and Tony was very popular. Everyone congratulated him and shook his hand. When the ceremony was about to start they all found their seats and waited for the awards to be given out. Tony wasn't the only one getting awards but he was one of the key ones that had done above and beyond his duty at work. Tom was standing up at the podium and was giving his long speech and then to Tony's surprise he had been offered a promotion and a better job there and everyone clapped. Tony was in shock and still went up to the podium and took his award. Tom sat down and Tony looked out at the crowd.

"I'm going to definitely say yes to that promotion. I can't turn that down in front of a whole room of coworkers."

Everyone laughed and he smiled at his wife.

"I just want to say thank you to everyone who has put up with me and has done as much work as I have on the accounts. I want to thank Tom for the promotion and for the award and for giving me the job in the first place. I also want to thank my wife Samantha for being the best wife and for sticking by me the whole time. I couldn't have done any of this without her. Samantha I love you and thank you."

Samantha blushed and could feel everyone starring at her but she didn't care she blew him a kiss and clapped with everyone else. Tony came down and kissed Samantha before he sat down. She was so happy for him that a happy tear rolled down her cheek. She really hadn't expected him to thank her like that in front of everyone but she was so happy that Tony and her were so much in love. She was still smiling even after the dancing and her feet were killing her. They had so much adrenaline going through them that they decided to go home it was only a few hours away. They changed and then got their car from the valet. They headed home.

"That was a really nice speech you gave Tony."

"Thank you. It was really because of you that I did all

that by the way. I pushed myself to make sure that I could provide for us and because you supported me. You know for some of the things I've done I have used some of your ideas so in a way I really did need to thank you. I wasn't expecting a promotion but I guess that was someone answering your prayers."

"I know and I'm very proud of you. I love you so much Tony."

"I love you too Sam and I'm so happy that we have each other."

They were talking a little bit when Sam saw something out of the corner of her eye and told Tony to stop. Tony pulled over and saw what Sam had seen. There was a car that had driven off the road and was wedged between two trees. Sam got out of the car and ran down there to see if there was anyone in it. Tony was now behind her and they both saw a woman in the front with her head on the steering wheel and since the front end was wedged between the two trees it was a little hard for them to get the car door open. When they finally got the door open Sam felt for a pulse and when she found one she told Tony to call the police. Sam was a nurse but wasn't sure she should move the woman just in case. She saw a lot of blood on the steering wheel and she kept checking her pulse until the police got there. After what seemed like forever the police showed up first and inspected the scene and they just thought that the woman passed out behind the wheel and that there was no foreplay here. The ambulance showed up and they got the woman out of the car. Sam wanted to go to the hospital and make sure that she was okay. She wasn't sure why she didn't even know the woman but she still felt like she wanted to know what was going to happen to her. They followed the ambulance to the hospital and Sam called Mike.

"Tony and I are going to the hospital."

"Why what happened? Are you both okay?"

"Yes we are fine but we found a car that had driven off the road and there was a woman pretty badly banged up in there and we are going to make sure she's okay."

"Why you don't even know the woman."

"I know but for some reason I feel like I need to make sure she's okay. Don't ask I can't explain it myself. Do you want to meet us there?"

"Why?"

"Because I want to see Ashley."

"Fine we'll meet you there."

Sam hung up the phone and looked over at Tony.

"I know call me crazy."

"I wasn't going to say anything."

"I just want to make sure she's okay that's all. I mean I don't know how long she's been down there and she looked like she lost a lot of blood."

"It's the nurse in you that's okay."

"I'm sorry if you want to go home you can just drop me off at the hospital."

"No if Mike is meeting us there then I'll just wait and see what happens and then maybe go home."

"Okay thanks Tony. I'm sorry if this isn't exactly how you wanted the night to end."

"No it wasn't in my thoughts but I guess in a way I want to make sure she's all right too. She looks kind of young. Do you think she had passed out at the wheel like the police think she did?"

"I don't know. I guess it's possible but it's just weird to me that a young woman with a bunch of suitcases and bags in her car would pass out behind the wheel."

"She may have been driving for a long time and didn't realize how tired she was and dozed off it happens."

"Yeah I guess so but something doesn't feel right and I don't know why. I guess we'll find out when she wakes up."

"Yeah I guess so."

Tony parked the car and they headed into the hospital. They saw Mike with Ashley sleeping in his arms and Tony took Ashley from Mike. Sam hugged Mike and she wasn't sure why but she started to cry. Mike looked at Tony confused and Tony only shrugged he was as lost as Mike was. Sam finally pulled away and looked at Mike while wiping her tears.

"Call me crazy but something doesn't feel right about her."

"You are a nurse Sam and I understand you want to help her but I think you have done enough to help her and now the doctors are going to do what they do best. I don't understand why you want to stick around?"

"I don't know something about the way the car was wedged between two trees and how much blood she lost makes me curious to find out if she's going to make it or not. I can't help it."

"So what did you need me here for?"

"I wanted you to sit here with me while Tony takes Ashley home. I just figured maybe you could help me figure her situation out."

"I'll sit here with you Sam but that's as far as it goes. I'm not getting involved with anything for a stranger."

Sam looked at Mike and then went and said her good-byes to Ashley and Tony. Tony left with Ashley in his arms. Sam sat next to Mike and waited for what the doctors were going to say about the woman's situation. They sat there for a few hours before a doctor came out.

"Are you the person that brought in the woman from the car that had driven off the road?"

"Yes how is she?"

"She's doing better now we got the bleeding to stop and she's going to live. She's resting still and her baby is going to live."

Sam looked a little surprised the woman didn't look pregnant at all.

"She's pregnant?"

"Yes. Do you know her?"

"No my husband and I were just driving by when we saw her car but she didn't look pregnant. I'm sorry I didn't mean to sound so surprised."

"Well she's only a couple months pregnant. I don't know if the woman even knows if she is pregnant or not. I guess we'll get some answers when she wakes up."

"Do you care if we see her?"

"Sure she's still sleeping but she should be waking up after the pain medication kicks in. Do either of you know her name or anything?"

"No wasn't her purse in the car with her?"

"No the police said there was no purse in the car but it was possible that it's there and they haven't found it yet. They finally got the car towed but because of the way the car was wedged they couldn't really do any real investigation."

"Thank you doctor."

The doctor walked away and Sam looked at Mike.

"Don't even think about it."

Sam shrugged and went to the woman's room and sat by the bed and watched her sleep. She didn't know why but she felt connected to the woman somehow and that was before she found out she was pregnant. She wasn't sure if it was because she had found her and felt like she needed to protect her or if she was more curious of what really happened. She looked up and saw Mike starring at her and shook his head and left.

Chapter 4

The woman had finally woken up and she didn't know where she was or what had happened. She saw a woman sitting in the chair and wasn't sure who she was.

"Your awake."

"Who are you and where am I?"

"You are in the hospital. My husband and I were driving by and saw your car wedged between two trees and we had you sent to the hospital. How are you feeling?"

"I don't know."

Sam noticed that she looked a little off but wasn't sure if it was because she was all drugged up or if it was because she was scared. The doctor came in and checked on the woman.

"How are you feeling today?"

"I don't know. How long have I been here?"

"Only a day. Do you know who you are?"

"Yes of course I do."

"What is your name?"

The woman tried really hard but for some reason she couldn't remember her name. She looked over at the woman and she didn't know what to say.

"You okay?"

"How come I don't know my own name?"

"Well from the knock on your head from the collision from the trees I would say you have amnesia. Things will start to come to you bit by bit though. Your motor skills and reflexes are doing fine. I'm going to keep you here for a couple more days to keep an eye on you but you should be fine. If you need anything let me know."

The doctor left and the woman just starred after him even after he was long gone.

"I'm Samantha by the way but you can call me Sam."

"Did we know each other before?"

"No this is the first time we've met."

"How come you are still hanging around?"

"I just wanted to make sure you were okay that's all. I'm sorry do you want me to leave?"

"No I'm sorry I guess I'm just really confused on what is going on. I can't really remember my own name and that's scary. I can't remember anything."

"Are you thirsty or anything?"

"Yes my mouth is parched thanks."

"I'll be right back."

Sam left the room and grabbed the woman a pitcher of water and a glass. She ran into the police on her way back.

"You were the one that found that woman weren't you?"

"Yes and she's awake now but she doesn't know her name or who she is or anything."

"Well we did find her purse it was shoved under the drivers seat more near the backseat. Her name is Julie Crawford and we found her address and along with all that we found several suitcases and bags shoved in the trunk and the back seat. She must have been traveling and fell asleep behind the wheel but the weird part is that she doesn't live far from where she had been driving. It looks as though from the gas tank and some other things on the car it looks like she had been down there for a few hours before you found her. She's lucky that you did find her when you did not many people stop for anyone these days."

"I'm just glad that we got to her in time. Was that it?"

"Yeah for now but when she starts to get her memory back we will need to ask her a few questions."

"Okay I'll keep you updated."

The police left her and she went back in the room. Sam gave her some water and then sat on the chair.

"I just found out that your name is Julie Crawford. Does that ring any bells?"

"No not really. How did you find out my name?"

"The police found your purse in your car and found some other things. Were you traveling or running from something?"

"I don't remember. I don't remember anything at all."

Sam stopped asking her questions it was clear she didn't know anything at all and they weren't going to get anywhere. She sat with Julie for a little while and then she was getting tired and decided to take a walk. She called Tony first and let him in on what was going on and then hung up with Tony. Mike had left the hospital and gone home after he saw Sam sitting with the woman. She called Mike.

"Hello?"

"Mike it's me Sam. I need you to do me a favor."

"No Sam I'm not getting involved."

"Mike she doesn't even know her own name. The police found some things of hers in her car. Her name is Julie Crawford can you just let me know where she lives please?"

"No Sam I'm not getting involved. I mean it."

"Mike you are the only person that can help me figure this out to help Julie figure out what happened."

"Why is this so important to you anyway?"

"I don't know why. Why were all those cases you did so important to you?"

There was silence and then Sam finally said something.

"I'm not asking much I just want to know where she lives."

"Why don't you ask the police they have her purse don't they?"

"Well yes but they said that she didn't live that far from where her car drove off the road and it still makes me a little uneasy that she doesn't know she's pregnant and doesn't know what happened. If she was running from someone I don't want them to find her."

"If she is running from someone then you shouldn't be getting involved. Why don't you just leave it's not like you owe her anything."

"Mike I saved her life and she doesn't know anyone or even who she is. I'm not just going to abandon her."

"She's a complete stranger."

"Yes and if Sarah was still alive and the shoe was on the other foot you would be doing the same damn thing I am right now. You can't tell me that you wouldn't be because I would know you were lying."

"Sam I'm not going to say not to do anything but be

careful. I'm not going to get in the middle of any of this I don't know her and I don't want to know her."

"Mike you aren't being fair."

"Why because I don't want to take a charity case? I don't know why you keep thinking she's running from someone maybe she was going to see a friend or her family and was more tired than she thought when she started to drive and she just dozed off. It does happen and I think you are putting way too much into this."

"Well for your sake I hope you are right and I am reading too much into it but for some reason I can't shake this feeling something is really wrong here."

"Why because she has amnesia?"

"No because she's acting very weird. It's like when someone quits doing drugs or smoking or whatever they start to get like paranoid and frantic. I don't know maybe it's just me from being a nurse for so long I can see things in her that aren't normal."

"Maybe she was a drug addict or something and maybe she's faking her amnesia to keep herself out of trouble."

"You think the worst in people you know that?"

"I'm just saying listen I have things I want to do today so if you don't mind I'm going to let you go now."

"Fine be that way but if you need me you know where to find me."

Sam hung up the phone with Mike and got her second coffee and then went back to see how Julie was doing. She saw the doctor and flagged him down.

"Yes how can I help you?"

"Did you do an alcohol test or drug test?"

"Yes and she came up clean on both accounts but that's how we found out she was pregnant. Since she has amnesia right now I think that telling her about the baby is probably not the best thing for her right now. We should wait until she starts to remember her name and stuff first."

"She knows her name now because I told it to her. The police were here trying to find out if she had woken up or not. They filled me in on her name and everything but I didn't tell her about the baby yet. I didn't think that it was my place."

"That's okay she should start to remember things on her own in the next couple of days."

"Do you think it's possible that she is faking the amnesia?"

"I don't see why she would. I mean she didn't really look like she was acting when she really couldn't remember her own name why do you ask?"

"I was just curious that's all. I really don't know anything about her but for some reason I want to know answers and I haven't really figured out why."

"You aren't the only one. The police want to know as well as I do to. I guess that's just the nurse in you."

"Well thank you doctor."

Sam went back to find Julie watching some television show and she was shaking a little bit like she would be if she didn't have a cigarette or drugs or something but it was weird if they didn't find any thing in her system. She sat back down and watched the television with Julie. Julie every once in a while would look over at Sam.

"If you don't really know me how come you keep sticking around?"

"I don't know I guess I'm just curious to find out what happened."

"Well it may be a long while before anything comes back to me. While you were gone I kept trying to rack my brain and figure out what happened to me. The only things I can remember are memories I think from when I was little but then again it might not be. I can't be for sure. Do you think any one knows I'm missing?"

"I don't know if anyone does they will know where to find you."

"I'm sorry for being rude to you. I guess I should be thanking you for finding me. The doctors said that if you hadn't been there when you were then I could be dead in my car right now."

"There is no need to thank me Julie. I was just happy I could help and that you were still alive. Do you know you are shaking?"

Julie starred at her hands and her legs kept twitching. She wasn't sure what was wrong with her and she started to freak out. That wasn't what Sam was expecting and called the doctor in to check on her. The doctor said that she was normal and there wasn't anything found in her blood or alcohol it was probably just her body reacting to the medication and the fact that she was maybe still in shock. It was a lot for her to take in and her body wasn't handling it very well. The doctor left and Julie asked Sam to stay with her and not to leave her alone. She was really scared and not sure why she felt Sam was safe and could trust her. After all she was the one that helped her and had made sure she was okay. She finally fell asleep and Sam stayed by her bedside. She called

Tony a couple more times and checked up on him and he said that he wanted her home soon. She said when Julie got out she would come home but not until then. She told him that something in her gut was telling her not to leave Julie alone. Tony thought she was crazy and it was because she was running on no sleep. Sam hung up with him and fell asleep in the chair while Julie slept.

Chapter 5

Julie had been in the hospital for a few days and was finally starting to remember things. She did finally remember that her name was Julie and that she was leaving but she still couldn't remember why or where she was going. Sam was still in the room with her and she smiled at Sam and then rubbed her tummy.

"I remember I'm pregnant or I was. Did the baby survive?"

"Yes the doctors said you both were healthy. Do you remember anything else?"

"No little bits and pieces here and there. I remember I was leaving for a reason but I can't remember where I was going and why I was leaving. The only guess I have is that it was because of the baby. I wish I could remember though. I remember my name and when I was born and where I was born. Those kinds of things are coming back but not the things that would be really important."

"Everything is important Julie."

"The doctors say I can leave anytime I want to but I don't even know where I live."

"Well we have an address on your driver's license."

"I guess then I do have a home."

"If you don't feel comfortable going back to your place Julie you can stay with Tony and I. We don't mind."

"Oh no I don't want to impose."

"You won't be. We have a daughter and she really needs me but I want to make sure you are safe and figure everything out before you go back home."

"Are you sure you don't mind?"

"No Julie your welcome into our house."

Sam and Julie both looked up and saw Tony with Ashley. Sam went over and hugged them both and then left Julie to get dressed. When she was done getting dressed she walked out of the room. Her legs felt a little wobbly but she was doing much better. Sam was holding Ashley and Tony wheeled Julie out of the hospital. They went back to their place and Julie looked around when she walked in. It was a nice house and Tony and Sam showed her around the rest of the house. They took her upstairs and showed her the room where she was going to be staying. The police had let Sam and Tony take Julies' bags and suitcases and they were sitting on the bed and the floor of the room. It was a nice room.

"This is where you are going to be staying while you are here. Make yourself at home and if you want you can take a shower. The bathroom is down the hall and we'll let you get settled. Ashley needs to be fed so if you need us we'll be in the kitchen."

"Thank you both very much for letting me stay here. If I get to be too much please let me know."

They smiled at her and left her in the room. Julie looked around and found drawers to put her clothes in and hung some of her clothes up. She didn't want to unpack everything just things she was going to need for a few days. She hoped that things would start to come back to her soon. She didn't feel right about staying here. She took some things out of her bags and brought a change of clothes with her to the bathroom. She saw the dried blood on her clothes and decided she was going to throw them away. They were ruined now and she didn't want to see that any more. She took a shower and she felt a lot better when she was dressed. She had left her hair down to air dry and put her things in her room and was going to get something to eat. She was close to the kitchen when she heard voices. She recognized Sam's but not the man's voice.

"Sam I can't believe you are letting her stay here."

"What do you want me to do?"

"I don't know let her go home where she will have familiar surroundings. That will help her remember things."

"She didn't look like she wanted to go home and besides I don't think she should go back until she remembers what happened. What if something happened back at her house and she goes back there?"

"Are you going to trust a stranger especially around Ashley?"

"Yes. She had a glow around her and it was the first time I've seen her smile when she saw Ashley. Listen Mike you may not trust her but I wouldn't put my family in danger if I didn't trust her. I trust Julie and she needs our help. Are you going to help her or not?"

"No I'm not. I told you I'm not getting involved with this."

"Then maybe you should leave. I don't even know why you came over here."

"I came over here to make sure she didn't do anything to you guys."

"Oh please Mike. This is my house and if Tony and I trust her then you should to. She's not going to do anything. She has her own baby to look after inside her. I highly doubt she is going to do anything to us."

"Fine but I don't want to have to say I told you so."

Julie hadn't moved fast enough and Mike saw her. She froze and they starred at each other for a few minutes.

"I'll leave and go back home if that's what you want."

"You can stay I don't care I don't live here."

Mike stormed out of the house and left Julie standing there. She was a little nervous going into the kitchen but she went in and saw Tony feeding Ashley and Sam making dinner. They both smiled at her when she walked in.

"Who was that?"

"That was my loving brother, Mike. I hope that he didn't say anything to you did he?"

"No but he doesn't trust me does he?"

"He doesn't trust anyone these days it's not you. Listen I'm sorry if you heard any of that. Tony and I trust you Julie so please stay and don't go back home until you remember things."

"Are you sure? I mean I feel like maybe I should go back to familiar surroundings like your brother said. It may help."

"I don't know Julie. I mean if you want to go home I'm not going to stand in your way but something tells me that there is a reason you didn't want to go home. I mean the look on your face when I said we have your address but I don't know."

"I have this gut feeling I was leaving home for a reason but I don't remember what it was. I guess I'm a little scared but then again maybe I was going to visit a friend or someone in my family. I just don't understand why I packed that much stuff to go visit someone. I mean if I remember correctly when you go on some kind of road trip you take a couple of bags of things with you not a closet full of clothes and all that personal stuff I found in my stuff. I feel a little safer here but I don't want to put anyone in danger if I was running from someone and they find out where I am."

"Sam and I will make sure you are safe Julie don't worry. If we thought you were going to put us in danger we wouldn't have offered to let you stay here. Don't worry we'll help you remember what ever it takes."

"Thanks that makes me feel a little better. I think."

Julie sat at the table and while Tony and Sam were making dinner Julie played with Ashley. She was making Ashley giggle and that made Julie smile. When dinner was ready they all sat down and started to eat. When dinner was done Julie offered to help with the dishes and let Tony take Ashley for a bath.

"Sam you have a beautiful daughter."

"Thanks. You know you are going to be a great mother."

"I hope so. Ashley looks a lot like you."

"Yes she looks like me but she has Tony's attitude."

Both of them started to laugh and finished cleaning up the kitchen. They decided to watch some television and then head off to bed. Julie was laying in bed and at first she was afraid to fall asleep. She didn't remember having any friends quite like Sam before her accident but then thought maybe she had but couldn't remember. She finally fell asleep and a little while later she woke up screaming. She sat straight up in bed and looked around and saw Tony and Sam both standing in her doorway and they turned on the light.

"Julie, are you okay?"

"I think so I just had a dream I think or a really bad memory I don't know what it was."

"Do you want to talk about it?"

"I don't know. I'm sorry if I woke you guys up."

"It's okay."

Tony left and Sam sat on the edge of the bed. Julie just looked at her and Sam knew she was trying to figure out if it was just a bad dream or if she really was getting her memory back slowly.

"I was getting into a fight with a man and I remember saying something to him and he hit me and then told me that if I left I would regret it. I remember driving and then when the car went off the road I woke up. I don't know what that was all about."

"Do you think that you were maybe in a fight with the man who got you pregnant and that's why you were running?"

"It's possible but highly unlikely. I don't remember telling anyone I was pregnant. I remember I found out from the doctor when I was only a few weeks pregnant but I can't remember if I told anyone or not. What if the man I got in the fight with had done something to my car to make me drive off the road or worse put me in the car and made it look like I passed out behind the wheel? I don't know Sam something about that dream seems so real."

"It might be some of the memories that have come back and right now they don't make sense but I bet in a couple of days it will start to make sense."

"I hope your right and I hope I remember before any one else finds out I'm still alive. I don't want to put anyone in danger."

"Don't worry just go back to sleep. We will figure this out."

Sam got up and turned the light out and left Julie in the dark. She lay back down but now she was really afraid to fall asleep. She lay there for a while but then she finally fell asleep again. She woke up and the sun was shining in her room. She got out of bed and she looked outside. She could see the back yard and there was a swing set as well as a pool. It was a pretty big back yard than what she thought it would be. She went into the bathroom and took a quick shower and then went down stairs. She grabbed herself some cereal and then started to eat. Tony came down stairs and was wearing a suit and tie.

"Are you going to work?"

"Yes. Sam will be here with you today until I get back and then she has to work the night shift at the hospital."

"She works at the hospital?"

"Yes she's a nurse. That's why she wanted to make sure you were all right after you were escorted to the hospital."

"Oh that would explain a lot then. Have a good day at work."

"Thanks. I'll see you later."

Tony left and Julie finished her breakfast. She decided to sit out back and get some fresh air and try and figure out what the dream had meant. She sat in the porch swing and starred out into the back yard.

Sam brought Ashley down stairs for her morning feeding and saw Julie sitting out back. She went into the kitchen and had gotten Ashley into her high chair when there was a knock on the door. She went and answered it.

"What are you doing here?"

"I come in peace. I've been doing some checking and found out a few things on Julie that might or might not help out."

"I thought you didn't want to help."

"I don't I wanted to check her back ground for your sake. It took me a while but I finally got what I wanted."

"What is that?"

"She lives in that big mansion looking house a few miles away from where she was in her accident. I checked out the place by driving by and it looks like she or who ever she lives with is loaded. Anyway the other thing I found was that the car was registered under her name and there isn't anything in her background out of the ordinary. Her parents both died when she was a teenager and she was an only child. That's about all that came up for her."

"See and you thought she wasn't trustworthy."

"Where is she?"

"She's outside right now why?"

"I was just curious I take it she heard what we were talking about in the kitchen last night?"

"Yes she did but she had a bad dream last night but she wasn't sure if it was an actual dream or a memory poking it's head out. I may have been right that something wasn't right and that's why she was leaving."

"Let's not get things confused from a dream and reality. Don't put things in her head let her figure those things out on her own, or you are really going to confuse her."

Sam heard the back door and saw Julie come running into the kitchen but she stopped when she saw Mike.

"I'm sorry I'll leave you two alone."

"No Julie what is it?"

"I just remembered something. That dream I had last night wasn't a dream it was real and I was leaving that man. We got into a fight about something that part I can't remember but I was leaving and he told me that if I left I would regret it. I waited until he was gone and packed up everything into my car and left before he came back. I remember driving and then for some reason I didn't feel real well and started to get dizzy and then I blacked out and the next thing I remember was waking up in the hospital. I don't remember what made me black out or anything but that has to help with something right?"

"Who was the man?"

"That part I don't remember but we were fighting about something and I wish I could remember what it was."

"It's okay Julie what you remembered is good. I hope I didn't put anything in your head last night about what happened."

"Oh no I didn't even think about what you said."

"Did it have anything to do with you being pregnant?"

"No I didn't tell anyone I was pregnant I told Sam that already. I need to lye down for a little bit my head hurts but I just wanted to let you know what I remembered just in case."

Julie left and went upstairs. Sam looked at Mike and he had no expression on his face.

"See I told you something wasn't quite right about her going back home."

"All right so you were right big deal. I'm going to do some more digging."

"Why are you wanting to help now?"

"I don't know something about what she said makes some sense I guess and it's weird that she would get dizzy and then blackout. Did the doctors do a drug test?"

"Yes and they came up with nothing and that was the same with alcohol. That's how they found out she was pregnant."

"Something doesn't make a whole lot of sense, unless the stress made her feel dizzy and pass out but I don't know about blacking out."

"Well let me know if you find out anything. I'm staying with her until Tony gets home from work and then I'm going to work. So she's not going to be left alone."

"I just hope I find out more before anyone else does. I mean if the man did do something to her car or something to make her black out then he might think she is dead and if he finds out she's not he might come back to finish the job and I don't want any of you in that situation. I've already lost one person in my life that I truly love and I'm not going to sit and watch it happen again."

Mike kissed Sam and Ashley and then left. He got in his car and headed back home. He wasn't sure why but something about Julie made him want to help her so that she didn't look so scared. She was attractive and he couldn't figure out why that was so important to him. He got out his lap top and started doing some more searching. He called his boss and asked if he could get a little help to figure some things out. She said she would help and was glad that he was caring about people again. Mike hung up and did some more checking. He didn't know why but something about Julie made him feel something and he wasn't sure what it was. She was young like Sarah but she had dark hair and she had the most beautiful hazel eyes. He saw how excited she was when she had remembered something but then saw the excitement go away and turn to terror when she was telling them what it was she remembered. What he couldn't figure out was why she would leave a place like that and if it was a husband or a boyfriend. He knew it wasn't a family member because she was an only child and her parents were both dead. Her mom died first in a car accident and her father died of cancer. He felt sorry for Julie that she had lost them both and wondered if she had just been living with a friend and finally couldn't take it there anymore or was it the father of her baby? Those answers he needed to find out if not for Julie for himself. He wanted to know what kind of danger she could be in and for some reason he felt as if he needed to protect her but from who and what? That was the question every one including Julie wanted to know and he was determined to find an answer out for them as soon as possible. After doing some more digging and coming up with nothing to go on his phone rang. It was his boss. He got the answer that he needed on whom the man was.

Chapter 6

Mike went over to Sam's to let them know what information he had found out. Tony was gone and at work probably and he saw Sam's car in the driveway. He knocked on the door and Julie opened it.

"Where's Sam?"

"She's sleeping. She came in later than she wanted to and was really tired. I'm watching Ashley. You can come in if you want to."

"How are you feeling today?"

"Much better but I figured out who that man was and I figured it out while Sam was at work. He's my husband. After I went to lie down for a little bit some more things came to me. I went through some of my stuff and I found a wedding band in my stuff as well as a wedding picture of us. The only thing is I don't remember what we were fighting about or why I was leaving him."

"Well I found out some information for you as well and since you know he's your husband I can skip that part. He's apparently worried sick about you and put in a missing persons report."

"Did you tell him where I was?"

"No I haven't done anything yet. I was hoping that you would be able to tell me some more information about him."

"I don't remember much about him. I saw the picture of us and some things came back like where we were married and I remember only being like nineteen when we were married but that's about all I can remember."

"Do you want to go back to him?"

"I guess I probably should. Whatever it was we were fighting about couldn't have been that bad I guess if he was worried sick about me and put out a missing report."

Mike wasn't so sure about that but maybe she was right. The fight may have been just a quarrel about something silly and she was upset and decided to leave and had totally overreacted. Women tended to do that these days but then a part of him wasn't sure about that either. He didn't know what to believe. He would obviously have to let her do what she wanted since it was her life and then he caught himself staring at her.

"Mike what are you doing here?"

"I was just talking to Julie. Did you sleep okay?"

"Yeah I needed a little nap. So what is going on?"

"I remembered who that man was. He's my husband and his name is David. We've been married for ten years and I still don't remember what we were fighting about. Mike told me that he was worried sick about me and put in a missing persons report so I guess I'm going to go back to my husband."

"Are you sure that's a wise decision? I mean if you don't remember what you were fighting about maybe you shouldn't go back until you remember what it was you were fighting about."

"No I mean it could have been something minor. I mean I am pregnant and since he didn't know that maybe my hormones were on overload that day and I overreacted. I mean if we had such a big fight why would he put out a missing persons report on me?"

"I don't know but something doesn't feel right Julie and I just don't feel safe letting you go back there if you aren't really sure what it was you were fighting about. I mean I can't make you stay here and I can't make you not go back to your husband that isn't my place to tell you what to do but I'm just saying if he tried to hurt you once before then what will make him not try anything again?"

Julie didn't get to say anything because there was a knock at the door. Sam answered it but for some reason Mike felt the need to protect Julie. He stood in front of her and there was a man at the door. It was David and there was an officer behind him.

"Is Julie here?"

"Who are you?"

"I'm her husband David. The officer said that she has been staying with you."

Sam wasn't sure she wanted him to come in but she really didn't have a choice because he was already walking in. He saw Mike standing in front of her and she wasn't sure what to do or say.

"Julie, honey it's okay I've come to take you home with me."

Julie stepped away from Mike and she looked at him and he looked like he hadn't slept in a few days. Something about his smile made her cringe a little and she was a little uneasy about going back with him but he was her husband after all.

"I'll go get my things and then I'll be ready to go."

Julie left and went upstairs. She was still mostly packed except things she had gotten out to use in the last couple of days and packed them up. As she was packing Mike had snuck up stairs to see if she needed any help.

"Do you need help with anything?"

"No I think I got it thanks."

"Listen I'm sorry we got off on the wrong foot that wasn't my intention. I'm just not a trusting man this past year so I don't want you to take it personal."

"I would have done the same thing had I been in your shoes and I didn't take it personal. Can I ask you a question? Do you think that David was capable of trying to kill me?"

"I don't know. I don't really know the guy. Why?"

"I don't know something about him doesn't feel right."

"Go home with him and if you still don't feel right call me or Sam someone will come for you."

"Thanks I think."

She looked nervous and Mike could tell she really wasn't sure she felt safe with this guy even though he was her husband. He helped her carry her things down stairs and David grabbed them from him and took them to the limo that was parked outside. Julie hugged Sam and Mike and told them to keep in touch and got in the limo. After the limo had pulled away and it was out of sight Sam finally closed the door.

"I don't trust that man."

"Why did he say something to you?"

"No just the look on his face and the way he acted. I don't know maybe I just wanted to keep Julie here. It's been a long time since I've had a girl friend to talk and hang out with. It's probably nothing but maybe you should do some more digging."

"I'm not finished don't worry. She told me that she doesn't feel right about him either but she said she should go with him. I told her that if anything should happen or she remembered what it was she was leaving for to call one of us and we would be there to get her. I am going to do some more digging and see what I can come up with and for David's sake he better not hurt her."

Mike left and didn't say anything else. Sam was a little surprised by that comment but brushed it off for now. She felt the same way though.

The limo pulled into the gates of a mansion. Julie looked from David to the house.

"We live there?"

"Yes we've been living there since we were married. You do remember us being married right?"

"Yes I remember. I'm remembering a lot of things."

"Do you remember the night of the accident yet?"

"No all I remember was blacking out behind the wheel and waking up in the hospital."

David helped her out of the limo and she followed him inside. It was huge and she couldn't believe that she lived there. David showed her around and then took her up to their bedroom. She remembered the rooms but couldn't put herself in them.

"Maybe you should get settled in dinner will be around six."

"Okay thanks."

Her suitcases and bags were sitting on the floor and she started to unpack things and was putting them away when there was a knock on the door.

"Come in."

The maid came in and asked if she needed any help with anything.

"Were you here when I left?"

"Yes ma'am."

"Do you remember what David and I were fighting about?"

"No ma'am. I was in the kitchen and you both were in the library. I'm sorry ma'am."

"It's okay thank you anyway."

The maid left and Julie started to unpack some more things. She sat on the edge of the bed when she felt a slight pain in her stomach. She hoped that the stress wasn't too much for the baby. David came in and saw her on the edge of the bed.

"Julie, are you okay?"

"I'm fine. Did I tell you I was pregnant?"

"No that's great how far along are you?"

"A couple months give or take. They found out when they did a drug and alcohol test. I just needed to sit down for a minute nothing to be alarmed about. Was there something you wanted?"

"No I was just checking up on you. I think that you need to take it easy for a little while you both have been through a lot and I think until you get further along that you stay in bed."

"I'm not going to stay in bed forever. I need to be finding out more information of why I left in the first place. Did we have a fight?"

"No why would you think we had a fight?"

"I don't know something about my packing practically everything I own into my car made me think we had to have gotten into a fight or something. That just doesn't seem normal."

"No I was at work most of the day and when I got home you weren't here. I thought maybe you had been kidnapped or something but then when the police took a report they said that you probably left willingly since all of your things were gone. I thought maybe you had a man on the side or something and ran off with him."

"No I would have remembered that."

"Well why don't you rest for a little while and I will bring up your dinner. You've had a rough few days and I want to make sure you are taken care of."

David had the maid come back in and put away the rest of her things and Julie took a shower and then got into some pajamas and lay in bed. She tried to fall asleep but every time she did she saw David hit her and then they were arguing. She wasn't sure that David was telling the truth though because the maid said that she saw them in the library but couldn't hear us arguing but Julie remembered David slamming a door and threatening her if she did leave him. She remembered being really upset and packing up her things but she still couldn't figure out what it was that they had been fighting about and right now she didn't care. David came in several times to check on her and had given her some food.

She ate some of it but was still not really that hungry but knew that in order for the baby to get the proper nutrients to grow she was going to have to eat more than that. She finally couldn't eat anymore and David had it taken away. He was now in his boxers and had gotten into bed with her. She lay on her side facing away from him and he put his arm around her. She didn't really feel safe with him for some reason. She finally fell asleep and decided not to worry about it. She was going to figure it out one of these days.

It had been a couple of months since she had been home and David had treated her like she was a queen. She was starting to warm up to him again. She was coming down the stairs when the house phone rang and she heard David pick it up. She got on the other phone to listen and she heard a woman's voice on the other end.

"I told you not to call me here anymore. She is back home and I don't want her to remember that you were the reason she was leaving me. If she leaves me you and I both won't get anything."

"When are you going to take care of the problem?"

"I will give it time. I want it to look like an accident so I have to wait until things die down a little bit. I don't want to get caught all right. I'll call you when it's time."

She hung up the phone and went into the kitchen and tried to act like nothing was wrong. She waited to be served her breakfast and read the paper. She heard David come into the kitchen.

"Good morning sweetheart. I have to leave to go to work in about an hour are you going to be okay here by yourself?"

"Yes I think I can manage. I do have to go to the doctor today so I'm going to have Sam take me if that's okay with you."

"That sounds great. Is there anything you need or want me to get on my way home tonight?"

"No I think I'm okay thanks anyway."

She hoped that she didn't seem nervous or anything to him. She didn't want him to know that she knew anything. She was going to have to play dumb for a little while until she could figure out how to tell Sam. She got up from the table and called Sam.

"Sam it's me. Are you busy today?"

"No what's the matter?"

"Nothing. David is going to work in a little while and I wanted to know if you could take me to the doctors to do my check up."

"Sure I'll come pick you up around eleven."

"Okay that sounds great thanks."

Julie hung up and jumped when she saw David watching her.

"Are you okay?"

"Yes you just scared me that's all. I'm still a little jumpy it's not you."

"So is Sam coming to get you then?"

"Yes. Are you leaving for work?"

"Not yet are you trying to get rid of me?"

"No I'm sorry I didn't mean for it to sound like that."

"Are you sure you are okay?"

"I'm sure."

Julie wasn't pulling this off very well she could tell by the look on David's face. She pretended that she cared about him and hugged him. He bent down to kiss her and as much as she didn't want to kiss the man she had to if she didn't want him to suspect that she was onto him. She shouldn't have listened to that conversation but it did help her remember what it was they had been fighting about. They kissed for a little bit and then he had to leave to go to work. She said she would see him at dinner. She watched him leave and then called Sam.

"I need you to pick me up now."

Sam didn't ask any questions and came to pick her up.

Chapter 7

Sam came to pick her up and Julie was quiet. They went to the doctor's appointment and every thing checked out okay. Julie got in the car and Sam started to drive her back to her house.

"Please don't take me back there right now. I need to talk to you about something."

"Is something wrong?"

"Everything is all wrong. I remembered what we were fighting about. He was cheating on me with some woman and I found out about it. I was going to divorce him and leave but he threatened me when I tried to leave. I waited until he was gone for about an hour and then packed up my car and left."

"Well that doesn't sound as bad as what I was thinking it was going to be."

"That's not all of it. I was starting to feel all right about David and then the phone rang. David answered it and I just happened to pick up and heard him talking. He was talking to a woman and he was telling her that she was the reason I was going to leave him and then she asked when he was going to take care of the problem. I would assume that it was me but now I'm confused because he also said that if I did leave him that they both wouldn't get anything. I don't understand."

"Okay now that part makes me nervous about you going back there. Maybe you should stay with us again."

"I can't Sam if he finds out that I know something he won't hesitate to kill me and right now I don't want to risk that because of the baby. The doctor said that I'm having a boy and he's very healthy. I don't want to risk the baby's life right now. I have to try and play this out for as long as I can. I just don't know how long that is going to be before he finds out that I know something. I mean I had to kiss the guy after what I heard and let me tell you how hard that was to pretend."

"We should tell Mike he would know what to do."

"No I don't think he really wants to get involved and I just didn't know who else to tell in case something does happen to me. I want someone I trust to know the truth. Sam you are the only friend I have right now and this is really hard to say but you are the only friend I have at all. I never had any friends before the accident and David made sure of that. You are the only person I trust anymore."

"Tony and I will protect you Julie you shouldn't go back to him."

"I'm not putting you guys at risk because I don't know what he's capable of doing. If he did have something to do with the accident I was in then he's capable of killing and I'm not going to feel right about putting you both at risk since you have Ashley. I should just go back."

"Not yet. Tony is at home he had the day off today and

he's making lunch. Stay for lunch and we'll talk about this okay."

"Okay but I'm still not sure it's a good idea."

Sam didn't really care what she thought to be honest because as far as Julie and her baby were concerned she didn't want anything to happen to either of them. If what Julie found was true then David was just waiting for Julie to mess up and know something. She didn't want David to find out and was afraid for Julie and her baby. She pulled into the driveway and got out. Julie was showing now and helped her out of the car. Tony was in the kitchen finishing up lunch when they walked in.

"Julie how are you doing?"

"Okay. I'm having a boy. He's a healthy boy too."

"You look much better. Are you hungry?"

"Yes I'm starving. How is Ashley doing?"

"Great. She's actually starting to try and crawl now."

"She looks bigger but she's still as cute as a button."

Ashley smiled when she saw Julie and Julie smiled at her. They all sat down to eat and Julie wasn't going to say anything more about David but Sam decided she was going to tell Tony.

"Julie was telling me that she remembered what it was David and her were fighting about now."

"Oh yeah what was it?"

Sam looked at Julie and Julie told her to go ahead.

"She said that she remembered why she was leaving David and it was because she found out he was cheating on her and she had wanted to leave. He threatened her that if she left she would regret it."

"Okay I don't get it why would you leave him if he was cheating on you?"

"That's what I said too but there is more to it than that. Julie you should tell him."

"Well apparently it wasn't the first time he had cheated on me and I warned him that if he did it again I was going to leave him. I was doing something I can't really remember what shopping or something and I saw him with some girl and they weren't just together they were kissing and groping each other on the street of all places. I confronted him about it later on that night and he denied it and said I was making things up. I went into detail and I could tell that he knew that I had caught him in a lie so he kept apologizing and said that it meant nothing. I told him that he had cheated on me for the last time and was leaving. I remember him grabbing my arm and slapping me and telling me to snap out of it. He could have whatever he wanted and there was nothing I or anyone else could do to stop him. He told me that if I tried to leave him that I would regret it and then he left to go to work. That night he was working the later shift so I had time to pack up everything I had and head out. I don't know what he did but he had to have done something to make me pass out behind the wheel or maybe he did something to my car and I thought I felt dizzy but maybe it was the car it had spun out of control and then I blacked out. I can't be for sure of that yet but then I was coming down for breakfast this morning and the phone rang. I went to get it but David had picked it up already and I heard the conversation. It was the woman that he had been cheating on me with and they were talking about if I left him neither one of them would get anything and then she asked when the problem would be taken care of; which I'm sure they meant me and he said that he would when the time was right. She was the reason I was going to leave him in the first place but what I don't understand is why he wouldn't get anything if I left him. He can have the whole damn house if he wanted it I just wanted to get out of there. I don't know where I was going and at the time I don't think I cared as long as I was away from him."

"Julie you can't go back there if he has a death wish for you."

"That's the thing though maybe if I act like I don't remember anything he won't try and kill me at all. I was starting to actually trust the man and now after that phone call it's hard to trust him. I played it off pretty well this morning but I don't know how long I can do that without him suspecting anything. I don't want you guys at risk and I don't want to risk my baby's life either. He's not even born yet and I'm being over protective."

She laughed a little to lighten the mood. Sam smiled at the joke and then started to think about what they were going to do.

"What if you stay with us? He won't be able to touch you Julie."

"Tony I'm not risking both of your lives and Ashley's to save mine. I already told Sam that and I don't have anywhere else to go. My parents are both dead and I'm an only child. I started to remember more things while I was at the house. Another thing that bugs me is the fact that when I got back the maid said that she saw David and I but we were in the library and she was in the kitchen. When I asked David about the fight he said that he was at work all day. He doesn't want me to remember the fight because he knows when I remember I'm going to leave him. He wants me dead instead of leaving him and that's what really scares me. I don't know what him cheating on me and me leaving have anything to do with why he wants to kill me. I don't understand why a husband would want to kill his wife."

"It's not safe for you there Julie and I don't care what kind of risk having you with us means. Sam and I are your friends and we aren't going to let you go back there. We will drive you back to get your things and then we are going to come back here."

"Tony and Sam I know you mean well but Mike was right in the beginning I don't want to risk Ashley's life or either of your lives and if I stay here he will find me. He knows where you both live and he knows that you both are my only friends. It won't take him long to find you guys and do what ever it takes to get to me. I don't think he wants to kill me until things die down a little because he wants it to look like an accident. I only wanted to tell someone so that if for some reason I end up dead you know it wasn't an accident and that it was deliberate. I had hoped that my gut feeling of going back there was all wrong but it was right and I shouldn't have gone back until I realized why I was leaving the bastard in the first place."

"You won't be risking our lives and Ashley can go stay with Mike for a while. I'm not going to worry about it we will work something out. Tony and I are going to take you back to your place to get your things. David won't be there will he?"

"No he should still be at work until around six that's when we eat dinner together."

"All right then we'll all go and then that way if David does show up we'll be there to witness anything but I doubt that he'll try anything if we are there."

"I hope you guys know what you are doing because I still don't like this idea."

Sam and Tony kept assuring her that everything was going to be okay. They got in the car and headed back to Julie's and Julie went inside alone. Tony and Sam decided to stay outside in case David came home. Julie went up to her room and started to pack her things again this time she wasn't going to pack everything just things she was going to need. She was carrying her bags out of the room when she saw David standing at the top of the stairs. She froze not sure what she was going to say to him or what he was going to do.

"Where are you going?"

"I was going to baby sit Ashley while Tony and Sam went out. I was going to call you before I left."

"Why do I not believe you?"

"What are you so afraid of if I leave you anyway?"

"So you do know why you were leaving then don't you?"

"No I just asked you a question. I'm not leaving you are the one freaking out that I was going to be leaving you."

"How dumb do you think I am Julie?"

"I don't think you are dumb David but I think that you worry too much. What were we fighting about the night I did leave?"

"We weren't fighting I don't know where you keep getting that idea from."

"Don't play dumb with me I know a little bit more than you think I do. You were cheating on me that was why I was leaving wasn't it?"

"You really don't know do you?"

"Know what?"

"I see that you don't so I'm not going to tell you but if anyone asks it was just an accident. You say you aren't leaving me but you are. Those are not over night bags."

"David you were cheating on me and I know you were doing it more than once and I warned you that if you cheated on me again that I was going to leave and that's why you did something to my car or made sure that I didn't leave you but what I don't understand is why what did I ever do to you?"

"Nothing Julie that's just it. You are so oblivious to the world around you that you don't see when you aren't pleasing your husband. I have to go other places to get it and you sit around here like you don't have a care in the world. I'm tired of this if you want to leave then leave."

Julie started to walk by the stairs and then she turned to look at him.

"And to think I was starting to trust you again I guess my gut about you the first time I saw you when you came to get me was right. I shouldn't have come home to you."

She turned and then she saw the stairs up close and personal and fell to the bottom of the stairs. Sam and Tony had wondered what was taking Julie so long so they left Ashley in the car since she was asleep and headed into the house. They heard the arguing and then it was silent and they went in and saw David at the top of the stairs and Julie was at the bottom of the stairs lying motionless. David saw them looking at him and came running down the stairs. Tony pushed him away from Julie and called for an ambulance. Sam knew she wasn't dead because she checked for a pulse and even though it was a little fainter than it should be she knew she was still alive. When the ambulance got there the police asked David tons of questions and Sam told them what she saw and then Tony and Sam left to go to the hospital. David was still being questioned especially since Tony and Sam had said that David pushed her down the stairs. When they got to the hospital Julie was being checked out. She was okay and so was the baby. Julie had just been knocked out but she was going to live and so was the baby. Julie smiled at Sam and Tony when they came in.

"How are you feeling?"

"Like I fell down a flight of stairs. Thank god you both were there or worse things could have happened to us."

"Well we saw him push you but we were too late so the police are questioning him some more. You will be safe in here."

"I don't know what I did to deserve friends like you both but what ever it was I did something right."

They all smiled and Sam and Julie started talking about baby boy names and what would a good name be since Julie didn't want to talk about what happened. She was tired of talking about David and how things could have ended up. She was looking for good and happy news. She had to stay over at the hospital for the night just to double check and make sure there were no other problems that the doctors couldn't detect right away but then she was free to go. Tony and Sam had suggested that she stay with them and they would get police to patrol the house more often especially if David wasn't arrested. Julie knew that David would find a way to get out of being arrested and say that she fell and that Tony and Sam didn't like him and was making things up. They weren't in there when it actually happened but only Julie and David knew that. Julie would have stood by them if she had been awake to talk about it but she wouldn't have sided with David. When Julie couldn't talk anymore Sam and Tony left her in her room to sleep and sat outside her door to make sure no one got in there.

Chapter 8

Sam got up from the seat and told Tony she was going to get some coffee and would be right back. She needed to stretch her legs were killing her from sitting. She used the coffee break as an excuse to call Mike; she knew that he would know what to do.

"Hello?"

"I'm in the hospital again. It's Julie."

"What happened?"

"She's fine. Listen Mike she needs protection and I don't know if Tony and I are going to be able to give her the protection she needs."

"Oh no, she is not staying with me."

"Why not?"

"Sam I know what you are up to and it's not going to work."

"I'm not trying to set you up this time I swear. David is dangerous and he tried to kill her by pushing her down the stairs. Thank god that Tony and I were there for her."

"What were you guys doing there?"

"She figured out why she was leaving David in the first place. She talked to me today when I took her to get her check up and she was so scared of going back there. She found out that he had been cheating on her and it wasn't the first time and when he threatened her that she would regret it if she left she waited until he was at work before she packed up her car and headed out. She doesn't know what it was that happened exactly with the car but she knows that David had something to do with it. She doesn't know why he would want her dead but she overheard a conversation with David and the woman he was cheating on her with and well let's just say it verified that he's a dangerous man and was out to kill Julie and if she leaves him then he doesn't get anything. I need you to get protection for Julie."

"I'm going to do some more digging then and get back to you all right. She will be safer in the hospital so just stay with her and I'll call you in the morning to let you know what I find out okay."

"All right but she's being released tomorrow so don't wait to long. I don't know if David was put in jail or not and I don't want to find out right now. I just want to make sure that Julie and her baby are safe."

"I understand I'll try and get something to you by morning. Just hang tight. If anything should change call me as soon as you know anything okay."

"All right. Talk to you later."

Mike hung up with Sam and started to get to work on Julie's background again. Why would David get nothing if she were to leave him and why would he want to kill her? He called his boss and told her the situation; she said she would do everything she could to get more information on Julie's background and to check the money status that had to be the reason for all of this. It was either that or greed but his bet was that it had something to do with money. He did his own searching and after a few hours of doing some digging he found out that it was all about money. Her father had left her over a few million dollars and the life estate. She sold the house when she was married to David and they had gotten the place they have now. He also found out that David was a very good physician and that he was pretty well off himself but not as much as if Julie was dead. His boss had dug up more information and according to his boss, Julie had a life insurance policy well over three million dollars. As long as David and Julie were married should anything happen to her, David got it all. Not only the money that was in the life insurance policy for Julie but the money that her dad had left her as well. If she left him he got nothing and that's why he wanted her back with him. When she started to figure things out he wanted to make it look like an accident. The falling down the stairs routine and once again that death didn't happen either. He shouldn't have let her go back with him especially since she said herself she felt like something was wrong when she saw David. He didn't want to make the same mistake he had with his own wife and this time he was going to make sure that Julie was protected. He had a couple of FBI agents waiting at Sam and Tony's and was going to make sure that David didn't touch any of them. He set up an alarm system at Sam's just to be on the safe side and then when he felt that it was safe enough he met them at the hospital. Sam and Tony looked so tired and Ashley was asleep in Sam's arms. He told them to go home and get some rest and he would take over watch. He filled them in on the security system and that he had some men watching the place just in case David decided to get ballsy. Sam and Tony left and Mike sat in the chair. He checked on Julie a few times and she looked so peaceful. He also noticed that she was now looking more pregnant and she still looked so beautiful. He closed the door and sat back down he wasn't sure why but he couldn't get her out of his mind. He wouldn't admit it to Sam or anything but in a way he was kind of glad that he was there to protect her. Then the more he thought about it he wasn't sure if it was because he wanted to protect her or if it was because he felt if he protected her then it would make him feel less pain for not saving Sarah. He didn't know and the more he thought about it the less he wanted to. He couldn't stop thinking about Julie and even when she was living with David he still had visions of her in his head. He dreamt about her and couldn't figure out why. She was a young attractive woman but no one had made him feel the way he was feeling right now and that included Sarah. He tried to get it out of his head and focus on watching out for Julie he couldn't risk messing this up. He got a call from Sam.

"We are home and the security system is on. If Julie should wake up before we get back there make sure she knows we are going to come back to get her."

"I will don't worry. Get some sleep the next few days or so are going to be rough."

"I know but at least I will know that she's safe. I still don't understand why she can't stay with you."

"No I got the security system all set up for you guys."

"I know but your place has much better security than a

whole country does but I don't want to fight with you tonight. I'm too tired. I'll see you in the morning."

"See you in the morning."

They hung up and Mike continued to watch the door. He would get up and check on Julie once in a while and one of the times he did he saw her moving around in her sleep. He knew she had to be having a bad dream or reliving one of the bad dreams that was reality. He went in and shook her a little bit until she opened her eyes.

"What are you doing here?"

"I'm watching you while you sleep."

"Where are Tony and Sam? Are they okay?"

"Yes they just wanted to get some sleep and I said that I would take over for a while. You are safe you can go back to sleep."

Mike turned to leave but he felt her touch his arm and it sent chills through his body. He turned around and looked at her.

"Please don't go. I don't know if I can go back to sleep. I keep seeing David pushing me down the stairs and every time I think I'm okay he's trying to kill me. I don't know why though."

"Don't worry about it Julie I won't let anything happen to you and neither will Tony or Sam."

"I'm sorry I got you involved in this Mike. I'm sorry I got Sam and Tony in this too."

"Don't be sorry it's not your fault. If they wouldn't have found you when they did you might not be alive."

"Maybe it would have been better that way."

Julie turned her head because she had a couple of tears

roll down her cheeks. He turned her head to look at him and wiped the tears with his thumb.

"Don't you ever think like that you hear me. I'll stay in here. Why don't you try and go back to sleep? You need to stay rested up for the baby's sake."

She rubbed her belly and smiled and then tried to go back to sleep. She didn't know why but she felt safe with Mike. He held her hand while she tried to go back to sleep. She wished that David would just go away and let her move on in her life. She knew that was never going to happen though and hoped that she didn't put anyone's life in danger by staying with them.

Chapter 9

Julie woke up and saw that Mike was still sitting in the chair and smiled a little bit. Mike smiled at her and stood up.

"How are you feeling?"

"Okay I guess. Thank you for staying."

Sam and Tony walked in and saw that Julie was awake and Mike was in the room with her.

"Julie how are you feeling?"

"Better I think. I just want to get out of this hospital."

They all laughed and got Julie released. They went back to Sam's and Julie sat on the couch. Tony put Ashley in the playpen and then sat on the couch as well. Mike was making sure that the security alarm was on and kept looking outside. Sam was standing next to him.

"Do you think he will try and get to her in here?"

"I don't know what he's up to and I'm not taking any chances."

Sam looked outside with him as well and then the phone started to ring. Sam went to go answer it.

"Hello?"

"Is she there?"

"No she isn't here David."

"I know she's there let me talk to her."

Sam looked at Mike and he told her to hang up the phone.

"Don't hang up on me Samantha. I just want to make sure she is doing okay."

"No you don't David."

Sam hung up the phone and went to go sit down when the phone rang again this time every one let it keep ringing. When Mike couldn't stand the phone ringing anymore he unplugged the phone. Julie looked scared but she didn't want to admit it to anyone. She felt restless and decided she was going to go in the kitchen and make something to eat she had to keep herself busy and wasn't sure how. Sam got up and went in the kitchen with her.

"Sam I shouldn't be here I should go back to him. He's not going to stop until I am dead."

"No Julie you are safer here. I'm not going to lose the only friend I have and besides that if he kills you then your little boy will never get to see life."

Julie rubbed her belly and sat at the table.

"Why don't you relax and I'll make you a sandwich."

"I can't relax. He's out there and god only knows what he's planning on doing next. I don't understand why I can't go somewhere else. He knows where you live and I don't want to put Ashley in the middle of any of this. I know you all mean well but I don't know what David will do next. I don't want to lose any of you guys."

"You are safer here than anywhere else and we have enough security that even the most professional won't be able to get to you. Mike is going to make sure of that."

Julie looked at Sam and she half smiled but she still didn't feel like she was completely safe. She ate her sandwich and then went up to her room. She sat on the bed and put her head in her hands. She didn't want to let anyone see how scared she was and crying in front of them just didn't feel right. There was a soft knock on her door and she tried to control herself but it was too late Mike had walked in. He saw her crying and he closed the door behind him and then sat on the bed facing her.

"Julie you don't have to try and stay tough. I know you are scared and I don't blame you."

"Yes I do. If I fall apart then every one else will have pity on me and I don't want pity or sympathy. I just want David to leave me alone. I don't even know why he wants me dead."

"I can tell you why. I found out more information while you were in the hospital."

Julie looked at Mike and was waiting for him to tell her.

"It's because you have a lot of money. When your dad died he left you quite a lot of money and his estate. However when you married David you sold the estate and moved into the house you were in. You are worth more dead than alive but he won't get any of it if you leave or divorce him. He's trying to kill you but make it look like an accident and the more you are here the more he's not going to be able to pull it off. That's why he wanted to make sure you had no friends or family. He's been planning this for a long time and just waiting for the right moment."

"This is all because of money?"

"Afraid so."

"What is this world coming to? How much does he get if I do die?"

"He gets more than three million dollars."

"Now I get why he said if I left him he got nothing and said he had to make it look like an accident. It's all coming back to me now. My mother died in a car accident and then dad died of cancer. He always told me that if he died I would be all right but I never knew what that meant until he was gone. I met David through a friend of a friend and he was so sweet to me. I was still young at the time but for some reason I needed him and he must have known. I've been married to the man for ten years and I guess his greed took over. He's always been power and money hungry. I got him through medical school and he's now the best doctor around. He makes really good money but I guess somehow he found out how much I was worth dead. I remember going to my attorney and telling him to make sure that David never finds out how much I was worth dead. I never wanted him to find out but I guess somehow he found out. I guess his fling on the side is after David for the money or they are in it together. I guess I should change my will and my beneficiaries before something happens to me. That way even if I die he still won't get anything."

"Do you want to do that today?"

"I better do it as soon as I can just in case. I don't know what he's capable of and I don't want to let him get what he wants. Do you think it's safe for me to be out there?"

"I'll go with you."

Mike wiped her tears from her face and she smiled at him. That smile did things to Mike he didn't know what to do. He stood up and held out his hand for her and they went downstairs. Sam and Tony were playing with Ashley on the floor and looked up when they saw Mike and Julie coming down the stairs.

"Where are you two going?"

"Well I figured if something should happen to me then I'm not going to let David get what he wants. Apparently I'm really well off and he would never have to work again if I die. Mike is going to take me down to change my will and my beneficiaries just to be on the safe side."

"Well you both be careful."

"Hold down the fort while we are gone."

"We will don't worry."

Mike held Julie's hand and made sure that he was protecting her while he got her in the car. He headed to town and went to her attorney's office. The attorney was in a meeting but she wanted to wait for him it was really important. Mike helped her sit down and then sat with her while they waited for her attorney. A couple of hours had passed and her attorney waved for them to come in.

"So Julie what brings you here?"

"I need to change my will and my beneficiaries on my life insurance."

"Is something wrong?"

"Let's just say it's for the best that I do this."

"All right but your friend there can't be in here with you when you do this."

"Mike I'm sorry if you wouldn't mind waiting for me outside."

"Sure I'm right out there if you need anything."

Julie smiled at him and he closed the door behind him.

"So I take it David found out somehow didn't he?"

"Yes and even though I don't have any family left I want Sam and Tony to have the money."

"Who are they?"

"They are the ones that found me when David tried to kill me the first time. They have been protecting me ever since then. Mike is Sam's brother and he is making sure that David doesn't find me alone we don't know what he's up to."

"I see. So how far along are you now?"

"Four months. If this little guy and I don't make it then I don't want David to get any of the money."

"Wise choice. To be honest I never liked the guy."

"Thanks Tim. You couldn't warn me of that when I was younger."

They both chuckled and Tim got her will and everything out. She looked everything over and put down that Sam and Tony were her beneficiaries and that if anything should happen to her that they would get all her money. She put in her will that Sam and Tony and Mike all were to inherit her estate. She signed the paperwork and made sure that everything was filled out so that Tim could make it legal before the end of today. She waited outside the office until Tim had made it legal and then she thanked him and they headed out.

"How did it go?"

"Good. Let's just say that Sam and Tony and you are my family now so you all will be well off if something should happen to me."

She saw the look of surprise in eyes when she told him

that. He helped her get in the car and then got in. His cell phone was ringing and he answered it.

"Hello?"

"Mike, David is here and he won't go away. He's already broken a few windows and trying to get in the house but he's not very successful. Are you on your way back now?"

"Yes we will be there shortly."

Julie looked at him concerned but he didn't say anything. They drove in silence and she knew why when they got there. David was throwing things into the windows and she could hear Ashley crying. David turned and saw Mike pulling into the driveway.

"You stay here and don't move. I'm going to take care of this."

Mike got out and locked the door behind him. Julie watched him walk up to David with his fists clenched at his sides. David backed up and said he just wanted to see Julie and that was it.

"You need to leave now or you will be arrested for trespassing amongst a million other things."

"Where is she?"

"I'm right here David."

"Julie?"

"David I suggest you leave. I'm not going to go back with you."

"Julie I'm sorry I didn't mean to hurt you. I just want you back with me please."

Julie turned her back to him and he was furious now and Mike could tell that if he hadn't been there that he would do something to Julie. He picked David up by his collar and threw him in the street by the limo.

"Don't come back or there will be more damage done to you."

David got in the limo and it left down the street. Julie tried to relax and leaned up against the car.

"You shouldn't have gotten out of the car."

"He just wanted to make sure I was still alive so I let him. Now he knows I'm alive and where I am. I don't want to put Ashley, Sam and Tony in the middle of this anymore. Please Mike can we go somewhere else? Anywhere else?"

Julie followed him inside and saw that Tony and Sam were now coming down the stairs. Julie hugged Sam and she was so sorry for her.

"I'm sorry Sam."

"Don't be sorry it's not your fault. Everything is going to be okay."

"Sam I need to talk to you in the kitchen for a minute."

Sam looked up at Mike and she let Julie go. Tony hugged Julie while Sam and Mike went into the kitchen to talk.

"Tony I'm sorry for putting you guys through this and I will make sure that everything is fixed up."

"Julie, don't worry about it everyone is safe and that's what matters."

Julie still wasn't sure she wanted to stay there and keep putting their lives in danger but she had no where else to go. Sam and Mike came out of the kitchen and saw Tony and Julie on the couch. Tony got up and stood by his wife and then Mike spoke.

"Julie you are going to come stay with me. Sam and I agree that it would be safer for you as well as them if you were to stay with me. David doesn't know where I live and even if he found out you would still be safer with me."

"What about Sam and Tony if I'm not here and David comes back."

"We are going to go on a little vacation until Mike calls us and tells us everything is going to be okay. We need the vacation anyway."

Julie stood up and hugged Sam and Tony before she followed Mike to his car. She never in a million years thought that Mike would let her stay with him. She didn't know why but she felt really safe with Mike and she didn't know if it was the hormones or not but she was attracted to Mike. They didn't have to drive very far to get to Mike's house and it was much bigger than Sam's house. Mike helped her out of the car and walked up to the house. He led her into the house and she saw that it looked like it had been remodeled recently. She looked over at Mike and he looked still unsure about this whole situation.

"Are you sure you don't mind me staying here?"

"I'm sure. I won't let him hurt you."

Julie followed him up the stairs to where she was going to be sleeping and told her that she should lye down for a little while. Mike went to turn and walk back down stairs when Julie grabbed his arm.

"Mike, thank you."

"You don't have to thank me."

"Yes I do. If it wasn't for you, Sam, Tony and I would be dead."

Mike turned to look at her and she saw the concern in her eyes. She was really scared and looked so vulnerable.

He couldn't stop himself when he leaned down to kiss her. When she returned the kiss he didn't stop but for some reason it felt right and wrong at the same time. Julie finally pushed him away and went into her room. Mike was still standing there even though the door was closed and finally went down stairs. He made some more phone calls and had extra FBI agents standing guard outside his house. They of course were supposed to not look suspicious. Mike took a cold shower and wasn't sure why but that kiss felt so right with Julie but he didn't know why. He couldn't get her out of his head. He quickly dressed and then went downstairs. He wanted to stay down stairs just in case. He wasn't sure if he was going to be able to handle having a woman under the same roof as him it had been a year and half now since Sarah and it felt strange but when he was with Julie he didn't think about her. His main focus had been making sure she was safe. He was finally back to his old self again.

Chapter 10

A few months had gone by and Julie was getting bigger now and Mike had taken her to her doctor's appointments and even gone with her to her classes. She had been surprised when he was actually in the room with her pretending to be the father of the baby. They were on their way back from one of her classes when his phone rang.

"Hello?"

"I think that you need to come to the office we found out some more information about what really happened the night of Julie's car accident."

"All right we'll be down in a little bit."

Mike hung up the phone and she could see his clenched jaw.

"What was that about?"

"You may have been right that the car accident wasn't an accident at all. We are going down to the station they have more information."

Mike saw her eyes get big. It had been a while since she looked scared and he hated seeing her scared. They pulled into the station and Mike helped Julie out of the car. They went inside and the police took Julie and Mike into a room and closed the door.

"Julie do you remember what you did before you got in the car?"

"I packed up the car and I had one of my bottled waters with me and drank some of that before I got in the car why?"

"Well when we did a drug test it didn't show up but according to more information that we dug up from David that he was out of the country a few months before your accident. We found out that since he's a doctor and can get drugs without any questions that he had access to get any thing he wanted including a drug called rohypnol."

"What is that?"

"It's what we call the date rape drug. It's odorless and tasteless and can be slipped into a drink without any detection. It can cause a person to get dizzy and black out and wake up not knowing what happened during the time that they took the drug; which would actually fit what happened to you. He must have slipped it into your water bottles not sure which one you would take and to cover everything he put enough of it in each of your water bottles."

"So my blacking out at the wheel and not remembering things was because of this drug?"

"Yes we think so. Do you remember where David was a few months ago?"

"He was on a conference thing with the hospital in another country but I don't remember where exactly why?"

"Well we think that since that drug is legal in other countries then he got it from there and brought it back to use on you. Can you remember anything else?"

"Not really when he came back he spent a lot of time with me and I started having blackout spells. It wasn't very often though and I thought it was from stress or something because the doctors could never find anything wrong with me."

"That might be when it all started then. We have some other things to do we just wanted to be sure that our thought process was correct."

The officer showed Mike and Julie out and they got back in the car. Julie looked frightened and Mike wanted to hold her close to him but knew that he needed to get back to the house. When they got there he helped Julie out of the car and they went inside. Julie just stood there not really sure what to do. She couldn't believe that her own husband had been drugging her and then it really hit her. That had to be how she got pregnant because she didn't remember the last time she slept with her husband. She must have a look of concern on her face because Mike was looking at her now.

"Julie, are you okay?"

"No Mike I'm not. My husband has been drugging me and the more I think about it something else just hit me. This baby might be his or it might not be."

"What do you mean?"

"I can't remember the last time I slept with David. I mean he was never home and I guess with the blackouts he stuck around but I never remembered anything from the time of the blackout to the time I woke up. Sometimes I would feel sore but I didn't ever think that my own husband would be raping me. What if he had someone else rape me so that it would look like I was sleeping with someone else?"

Julie couldn't help but let a few tears fall down and Mike didn't know what to say to her. He wrapped her in his arms and let her cry. He picked her up and carried her upstairs and put her on the bed. He closed the door and went down stairs and called Sam.

"Are you okay, Mike?"

"No I need help with Julie. We just found out more information on that accident. She was being drugged by the date rape drug rohypnol and he must have been giving it to her for a while because when it was finally out of her system it would explain why she was acting so weird. She thinks that either her husband was raping her or David had someone rape her several times when she blacked out and I don't know what to do. She's resting right now but she's very upset."

"All you can do is be there for her Mike. She's very emotional not just with the new information but she's pregnant."

"Thank you that helps out a lot."

Mike hung up with Sam and didn't know what to do so he decided to make something to eat. He was starting to get hungry and knew that Julie had to be hungry. He was in the kitchen when he saw Julie coming down the stairs. She sat at the table and watched him making dinner.

"Have you ever been married?"

"Yes I was once."

"What happened?"

"She was killed."

"Oh I'm sorry I didn't know."

"It's okay it's been a little over a year now so I'm better about it."

"Can I ask what happened?"

"She and I were on a vacation working on our marriage and she was killed. I should have been able to save her but I wasn't fast enough."

He looked at Julie and she at first was looking at him and then looked at the floor.

"I was working with the FBI and after Sarah's death I quit. My job took me away from her and when I couldn't protect her I figured I didn't want to risk anyone else's life."

"Then why are you protecting me?"

Mike didn't know how to answer that because he wasn't really sure either.

"I'm grateful that you are if that means anything. I never thought in a million years that I would need protection against my own husband."

Julie smiled at Mike and he put the plate of food in front of her. They ate in silence and then he cleaned up the kitchen. He started a fire in the fireplace and she watched him. She sat in front of the fire and starred at it.

"My mother used to tell me that things happen for a reason and in a way I'm glad that you and Sam were there for me. I've never had many friends and even the ones I had didn't stay close when David was around. You guys are the only friends or family for that matter that I have."

"Why did you marry David if you weren't really happy with him?"

"When I lost my dad I didn't have anyone to turn to. David was there for me and I guess I thought I needed him in my life to feel complete. He was really sweet to me when we were first married but after he became a respected doctor our marriage started to fall apart. I saw less of him and we always fought. When I found out he was cheating on me I threatened to leave him and we were fine for a while but I gave him a second chance because I didn't believe in divorce. I still don't but I'm going to have to if he's going to try and kill me. I worked so hard to keep peace in our marriage but the more time went on the more we drifted apart. I guess I wasn't satisfying him the way he wanted me to and had to go to someone else for it. I found out I was pregnant but I never told him and when I left him that night I didn't know where I was going to go but I had to get out of there. I didn't trust David and I couldn't take it anymore."

"You did the right thing."

"I hope so. I was only thinking of the baby and I guess in a way I knew that I could find better. I just can't believe I stayed with him for ten years."

"I'm glad that you aren't with him anymore."

Julie looked at Mike when he said that and they locked eyes for a little while. Mike got on the floor with her and starred into the fire with her.

"That sounds like my marriage. I spent so much time working with the FBI that I forgot about my wife's feelings. We were trying to work out and took a little vacation but it didn't last long. Sarah was shot down right in front of me and hit by a car. I couldn't do anything to protect her and for the longest time I never forgave myself. I guess I took your case because there was something about you that I wanted to help. I can't explain it really but after I saw the look on your face when you saw David I just knew that I shouldn't have let you go with him. I blamed myself for you getting hurt again and I guess that's why I wanted to make sure you were safe.

If I have you in my sight at all times I would feel better about you being safe."

Julie looked at him surprised by what he was telling her. She felt the baby kick and she took Mike's hand to her stomach. He felt the baby kick and saw the smile on her face. He couldn't resist kissing those lips again and as much as he wanted to hold back he couldn't help himself. His lips were longing for hers. He bent down and kissed her lips and she didn't pull away right away but then after they shared a few kisses she pulled away.

"I'm sorry Mike I can't do this right now. I just want to wait until my divorce is over and David is out of my life. I'm sorry."

"Don't be sorry I shouldn't have done that. You are still a married woman and I'm sorry."

Julie didn't really want to stop kissing Mike but knew that she better stop. She didn't care if it was considered cheating on David or not because as far as she was concerned they weren't together anymore. She felt something for Mike and she wasn't quite sure if it was because he was there for her like David had been or if it was because she really felt right with him. She didn't want to get confused and mixed signals so she tried not to think about it. She just enjoyed the time she spent with Mike. They talked for a little while longer and then she was getting tired. Mike helped her up the stairs and made sure she was comfortable before going down stairs.

Another month had gone by and there was still no sign of David. Julie had decided that she better get the divorce papers sent to him before the baby came and Mike was sure that those papers would bring David back out of hiding. Mike had been going with Julie to her classes and he was getting good at coaching her. On their way back from class they were going to be stopping by her attorney's office to get the divorce papers that had to be served to David but she wanted to look them over one last time. She was sitting in the office and this time Mike was in there with her. She looked it over and made sure that David didn't get anything. She gave it back to Tim and she half smiled.

"I guess this is it. It's going to be final and there is no turning back."

"You are doing the right thing Julie. David will get over it."

"I wouldn't be so sure about that Tim. I haven't seen him in the last few months but I'm sure that those papers will bring him out of hiding again. I just wanted to check and make sure that he didn't get anything from me. I just want this to be over with."

"It will be before you know it. How is the baby doing?"

"Fine he's a little kicker though. Thanks Tim for all your help I really appreciate it."

"It's no problem your father and I were really good friends and I promised him I would look out for you and I think I've done a good job."

Julie smiled at him and got up. Mike and Tim shook hands and they walked out of the office. They were on the way back to the house when she felt another kick.

"He really is a little kicker."

"His he kicking you again?"

"Yes. It's like he wants to get out of me or something."

They both laughed and headed into the house. Julie went upstairs to take a shower and relax. Mike decided to make them lunch and waited for Julie to come down stairs. He put lunch on the table but she still hadn't come down stairs. He went up to see what was wrong. He found her sitting on the edge of the bed holding her belly.

"Julie is everything okay?"

"Yes I just got a cramp that's all. It's finally passing I'm sorry I didn't mean to worry you or anything."

"No it's fine. I'm just glad that you are okay."

Mike helped her up and helped her down the stairs. She saw that he had made them lunch and she sat down.

"So when do you think David will get those papers?"

"Soon. It's only a matter of time before he finds you."

"I know and I don't know why but it scares me to death."

"I'm not going to let him hurt you Julie. I promise you that."

"I know I trust you Mike. I just don't trust David."

Mike put her hand in his and she smiled at him. She knew he was trying to be nice and she knew that deep down inside she really did trust him with her life. They finished eating and decided to watch some television. Julie must have been tired and passed out on Mike. He picked her up and carried her up to her room and closed the door. He was getting used to her being around and was hoping that in a way this would drag out a little while longer but he knew deep down inside that it wasn't. It was only a matter of time before David did find out where she was staying and he came looking for her. He wasn't going to like the fact that she was going to leave him. Her mother was right in a way that things happen for a reason. If Sarah was still alive he knew that he wouldn't be able to protect Julie and he didn't know why that was so important to him but it was. He made sure that everyone was in place outside and kept a sharp eye out on the place. Mike made sure the security system was armed and decided to sleep on the couch this time.

Chapter 11

There was a knock on the study door and David told the person to come in. The butler handed him some papers and left. David looked at it and knew exactly what it was. He wasn't very happy at all. He knew that he was going to have take care of the problem one-way or another but wasn't sure how yet. He knew that Julie was being protected by that ex-cop and wasn't sure he was going to be able to get past him. He was going to have to take the chance. He made a phone call.

"I'm going to take care of the problem tonight."

"It's about time I was beginning to think you were never going to do it."

"Veronica, baby that money is going to be ours. I just need a few days after this problem is taken care of and we'll be home free. Don't try to contact me. I will contact you when it's clear."

"All right but I'm only giving you a week to call me."

David rolled his eyes and hung up with her. He had to get his plan into motion but wasn't sure how well protected Julie was. He didn't want to go in there himself but he knew that was the only way he was going to be able to take care of the situation. He had to shoot her and his alibi was that he was with Veronica all night. He knew where Julie was staying but getting on the property without being spotted was going to be tricky. He figured out a plan and waited until two in the morning to go through with it. He figured by then everyone would be sleeping and wouldn't hear him come in the house. He parked his car a few blocks away and went through the back yards. He knew that the house was being watched so to make sure he wasn't caught he decided to go around back and crawl through the basement window. He got in through the basement and was quietly coming up the stairs. He slowly opened the door and the house was pitch dark except the light coming from the kitchen. He checked out the down stairs and didn't see anyone so he headed up the stairs. He felt something on his back and turned to see Mike standing there with his gun to his back. David slowly backed down the stairs and turned to face Mike.

"So we meet again."

"Did you really think I was going to let you have her?"

"David she's not yours and by the looks of things it seems that you got the divorce papers."

"If it wasn't for you and your sister she wouldn't have divorced me."

"No but she had tried to leave but you wouldn't let that happen would you?"

"I guess you've done your homework then. I loved her but she's so needy all the time. One thing after another and I just couldn't take it anymore."

"So when she wanted a family and you didn't is that why you started drugging her? No wait you didn't want to be the one that actually raped her so you had someone else rape her so that she wouldn't know anything. You would be there for her when weird things were happening to her. You are a really sick bastard you know that."

"You have a thing for her don't you?"

Mike didn't answer just kept the gun pointed at David.

"Is this how you thank Sarah for always standing by your side?"

"Shut up."

"What are you going to do shoot me? I don't think you have it in you to shoot me."

David knew that he had gotten to Mike and kicked at Mike and hit him a few times until he wasn't moving and then went upstairs. He saw Julie sleeping and pointed the gun at her. He shot three times and smiled. He went over to make sure he had gotten her this time and noticed that it wasn't her under the covers it was a doll and other blankets shoved under the covers to make it look like she was sleeping there. He heard a noise behind him and saw Julie trying to get out of the closet.

"Nice try Julie. You almost had me there."

Julie froze not sure what to say or what to do. Finally she found her voice when she saw the gun being pointed at her baby.

"David you can kill me and the baby but you still aren't going to get any of the money. I changed everything and you are no longer my beneficiary and you won't get anything because I took you out of my will. If I don't die of natural causes even though we are still considered married then you still won't get anything."

"You are lying."

"No I'm not. That day you were trying to get to me at Sam's house and I showed up that's where I was. I was out changing my will and my life insurance policy. You can still kill me if you want to if you don't believe me but you won't get away with any of it."

"We'll just see about that."

She heard a gunshot and since her eyes were closed and she didn't feel anything hit her she opened her eyes. She saw David on the floor and Mike standing there with his gun. He had saved her. Mike made sure he was out and then the rest of the cavalry came in and took David away. Mike held Julie and she held him back glad that it was finally all over. After everyone was gone Mike sat next to Julie on the couch.

"How did you know he was here?"

"I heard a commotion down stairs and when I saw you with David I had to think fast. I just hid in the closet and thought that I would be able to sneak out of the room but it's a lot harder to move around when you have a baby in your stomach."

He smiled at her and she laughed. They were both thankful that it was finally over and that David was going to be in jail for a very long time.

A few months had passed since David was put in jail and Julie had insisted on going back to her house. She threw away anything that David had bought for food and did her own shopping. She had the maid get her new things for food and the butler helped her get rid of David's things. There was a time when she would have been upset that she had to leave David but not anymore. She had gotten a phone call from Veronica and she was surprised to hear that David was in jail and that Julie was still alive. Veronica was put in jail for conspiracy of murder. Julie had finally gotten her life on track. She had seen Sam and Tony a few times a week and they either went over to her house or they invited her over to theirs. She had seen Mike a few times since then too but not as much as she had been hoping for. She was going to be delivering the baby in less than a month and she was hoping that she wasn't going to be alone when it happened. She really had hoped that the kisses between them that it had meant something more than vulnerability or the needing of each other in a crisis situation. She hoped she had been wrong about it being those feelings but she couldn't get Mike out of her head or her heart and her stomach did flip-flops when he was around. He still took her to the classes and her doctor's appointments but they didn't talk as much as they used to and she wondered if now that she wasn't in danger if he wasn't interested in her anymore. She didn't want to think about it and was just going to live her life and worry about her baby instead of a love life. Sam had picked up Julie to go baby shopping. Tony and Sam had helped Julie fix up a nursery and she wanted to finish shopping before the baby came.

"I think that you shouldn't be left alone until after the baby is here."

"I'm not alone. The maid has been helping me and so has the butler. They've been a big help with getting things ready for the baby. I've been good on bed rest too but I just wanted to finish this one last shopping spree before the baby comes. Don't worry so much."

"I can't help it. I just don't want you to go into labor and there isn't anyone there to take you to the hospital."

"I'm not going to stay with you Sam so don't even think about it."

"You are as stubborn as Mike is."

"Well then I guess we have something in common then."

Julie smiled at Sam and Sam just rolled her eyes at her. They pulled into the parking lot and they got out. They were shopping for a while and then Julie needed to sit down so they decided to get lunch.

"I am having so much fun going through baby stuff."

"Well next week Tony and I decided to have a baby shower for you and we have a special present."

"Oh I can't wait."

"Are you sure you don't want to stay with us?"

Julie didn't answer but gave Sam a look and Sam knew she wasn't going to stay with them at least not yet anyway. After they were done eating and finished up shopping they went back to Sam's to have dinner and hang out for a little while. They talked for a little while and then moved to the living room to finish talking. Mike had stopped by for dinner and was still there when dinner was over. He usually left shortly after dinner so Julie thought it was odd he was still there. Sam and Tony came out into the living room and they sat down.

"Are you sure you don't want to reconsider staying with us until the baby is born?"

"What is this are you all going to gang up on me until I say yes?"

"Pretty much."

"All right but I don't have to like it. I will tell you guys that I won't be able to climb the stairs anymore. I think this little boy wants to come out now."

"I hope he doesn't just yet we haven't had the baby shower yet."

"Well I think he's been wanting to come out for a long time now."

They all laughed and continued talking. Julie was getting tired and Mike had stayed until she fell asleep.

It had been a week since she was conned into staying at Sam's and Mike had been over a lot more. Tony and Sam were both at work and Mike was watching Ashley so that she didn't have to worry about taking care of her. Julie sat on the couch most of the time and she started to get contractions but at first they were just slight pains. Mike called Tony's mother to come get Ashley when Julie first started to feel them just in case he had to take her to the hospital. Julie got up to get something to drink when Mike was outside with Tony's mother and when she stood up she felt something wet in her pants. She knew it was time the water just broke. Julie starred at Mike when he came through the door.

"What is it?"

"My water just broke. We need to get to the hospital."

"Talk about perfect timing."

Mike helped Julie get in the car and coached her on her breathing while he rushed them to the hospital. He kept telling the baby to hold on until they got there. When they got there Julie was rushed into a delivery room and Mike ran into Sam and she knew that it was time.

"Where is she?"

"In the delivery room."

"Where is Ashley?"

"I called Tony's mother to come get her when Julie started to get contractions. She had just left when Julie's water broke. You should be with her."

Mike called Tony and let him know that it was time and that Ashley was with his mother. He was on his way there and Mike was pacing the waiting room. Sam came out and looked at Mike. She walked over to him and he met her gaze.

"Is every thing all right?"

"She wants you in there with her."

Mike looked at her surprised and she smiled at him. Mike went in there and was coaching her the whole way through the delivery. A few hours of holding her hand and the pushing she finally had the baby. He was healthy and cried as soon as he came out. The doctors washed him up and let Julie hold him. She smiled at him and she was so happy.

"Did you name him yet?"

"No I never did find a good name for him."

"Why don't you call him Cole?"

"I like that name. Where did you get that name from?"

"That's what Sarah and I were going to call our baby boy if we had one."

Julie smiled and said that she was going to name him Cole for Mike. He left and gave Sam and Tony the good news. They were moving Julie to another room and were going to put the baby in the baby room to make sure he was all right. Sam and Tony saw him when Mike pointed Cole out.

He was the cutest little baby boy. They wanted to keep Cole in for a couple of days since he was a little earlier than what was expected but as far as the doctors could tell there wasn't anything wrong with him. They just wanted to be sure. Julie was finally in her room and was resting when Sam, Tony and Mike came in.

"She's resting we should come back later."

"No I'm not I was just resting my eyes."

They all looked at her in surprise.

"Did you guys see him?"

"Yes he's so cute."

"I can't believe he came early. Sorry we didn't get to have the baby shower."

"Don't be sorry. We will still give you the surprise anyway."

"So what is it?"

"We can't tell you. When you get back to your house you will see it."

Julie glared at them and smiled. She was feeling much better but after being in a few hours of labor she was more exhausted than she thought. The nurses brought the baby in for his feeding and everyone left. Sam and Tony left to get some coffee and Mike hung around until Julie was done feeding the baby. The nurse came out and said that he could go in now. Mike walked in and saw her smiling and talking to Cole. He wasn't sure why but he really was happy that she was okay and that her baby was fine. She looked like hell from delivering the baby but somehow she still took his breath away when he looked at her. He didn't realize he had been starring at her for so long when he caught her eyes on him.

"Do you want to hold him?"

"No that's okay. He's a beautiful little baby boy."

"Thank you. I couldn't have done this without you though."

"Why did you want me in the delivery room?"

"I needed your support. You were the one with me in all the classes and everything and Sam was making me nervous. I asked her to get you because you were always so calm and I needed calm. I'm sorry if I made you feel uncomfortable."

"No I actually enjoyed it. I was just surprised that's all."

"Are you sure you don't want to hold him?"

"Are you sure you want me to?"

"I trust you Mike."

Mike picked up Cole and held the little boy in his arms. He felt right in his arms and then Sam and Tony came in. Sam saw how content Mike looked with Julie and the baby. She really hoped that the two of them would end up together and she knew she was hoping for too much but she knew that Julie made Mike happy. She had noticed his mood go back to being a depressed one when Julie went back home. She invited him over every time Julie was over and he would light up when he saw her. She knew he missed her and was happy when she was around. Something had happened between them while she was with him. She and Tony left after a while to let Julie sleep. Mike was going to leave too but Julie wanted him stay. He watched her sleep and she looked so peaceful. He felt really content being there with her. It was like she put a spell on him or something every time he was around. He couldn't ever take his eyes off of her and stop making the feelings he was feeling for her go away. Even after she left he still felt like a part of him was missing without her being around.

Chapter 12

The next few days Cole had been very healthy and the doctors saw no reason for her stay any longer and let them go home. Mike drove her home and Julie saw that Sam and Tony were there. Mike grabbed the baby stuff and Julie carried Cole inside and she saw signs and Sam and Tony by the stairs. They ushered her upstairs and she was told to look in the nursery. She saw that the room was completely finished and there was a crib and a rocking chair in there for her. She didn't remember the rocking chair and then there was a picture of everyone and the baby in the room. She smiled and put Cole in his crib. He had fallen asleep and she couldn't believe how wonderful the room looked. She turned around and saw them all standing there looking at her.

"Well what do you think?"

"You guys changed it I see. Is the rocking chair new?"

"Yes that was the surprise but then we found out that the room wasn't completely done so we decided to finish it for you."

"Thanks you guys this means a lot to me."

Julie hugged them all and then decided to go downstairs with the baby monitor so she could hear if Cole cried. They went into the living room area and they sat down. Julie felt weird being in this house all by herself.

"You know I've been thinking. This house is way to big for me to live in here by myself and wondered if you and Tony would like to switch me houses."

"Are you serious?"

"Sort of. I'm really not that comfortable living in this big house by myself. I know that I have help but for some reason this house seems way to big for Cole and me. I was thinking of selling and getting something a little less big. I guess I should have thought about that before you guys finished the nursery."

"What if we all moved in here?"

"Oh no I don't think you guys would want to do that would you?"

"Tony and I wouldn't mind and then when Cole gets a little older Ashley would have someone to play with. If you aren't working you could baby-sit Ashley for us. We all would be in close quarters."

"That's up to you guys I guess we could work something out. I do have another half of the house that no one lives in. The maid and butler quarters are not even in the house. I don't want to feel needy or pushy or anything."

"Heavens no Sam and I could use a bigger house."

They started laughing and decided that Tony and Sam were going to move in with Julie and Cole. Tony and Sam left to check out the part of the house that they would be living in and Julie looked at Mike. She wasn't sure what he was feeling right now and she wanted him so bad to say that he wanted to live with them too.

"Mike the reason I wanted you in the delivery room is because you have been more of a husband to me than my own husband was. I was hoping that you would want to be part of the family but I don't want you to feel like you have to."

"I think that maybe it's too soon for me. I'll have to think about it for a while. I just don't want you to feel like you need me because I was there for you just like David had been there for you. I want you to be sure that it's something you want before we do anything."

Julie didn't get to answer or say anything because Tony and Sam had come back. They talked about when they were going to move in. They left and Julie was left alone and then she heard Cole crying. She went up to his room and sat with him in the rocking chair. She hadn't realized how much she really wanted to be with Mike. He was attractive and was there for her. Maybe he had a point maybe she only felt attracted to him because he had been there for her when David was trying to kill her. She didn't know what to think. She made Cole laugh and she decided she wasn't going to worry about it and she carried Cole around. When he had fallen asleep she finally decided to take a shower and change into her pajamas. She was getting into bed when she heard Cole crying again. She got up and checked on him. She picked him up and carried him around the nursery for a little while then sat in the rocking chair and he finally fell asleep again. She was going to put him down when he started to cry again. She decided she was going to be sleeping in the rocking chair. She knew that she was really going to be sore tomorrow after sleeping in the rocking chair but it was the only way Cole would sleep. She finally dozed off and tried not to dream about Mike.

It had been about a week since Sam and Tony had moved in and there was still no sign of Mike. He hadn't called or stopped by. Julie was thinking that maybe she was wrong about him. Sam and Julie had taken the kids out back and were sitting out in the middle of the yard. Sam was telling her something but Julie wasn't listening and had drifted off somewhere else.

"Did you even hear what I just said?"

"What I'm sorry no. I haven't been sleeping well and I tend to doze off with my eyes open. What did you say?"

"I said you should try calling Mike. He misses you."

"Right that's why he can't call me or stop by. I think I should just forget about it Sam. He was right maybe I thought I was in love with him because he was there for me like David had been there for me. I don't want to hurt Mike and I don't want to hurt again either."

"Well you must have done something to him because he started working again. That's probably why you haven't heard from him. He's been working on case after case and has been doing a really good job."

"Well I'm happy for him. Do you mind watching Cole? I am a little more tired than I thought and I don't want to drop him or anything."

"Sure."

Julie handed Cole to Sam and went inside and went up to her room. She wasn't sleeping because Cole wouldn't sleep in his crib and she didn't feel comfortable in the rocking chair. She lay on the bed and passed out almost immediately.

Mike had been thinking really hard about what it was he was feeling for Julie and he wasn't sure if it was really love or if he felt that she had saved him from losing himself completely. He had gone back to work and had been successfully solving cases one by one and he didn't know if it was because of Julie or if it was that he was finally back on the saddle. He was finally over Sarah and had solved three cases within a week and it was a good thing. His boss was glad to have him back and she noticed a different glow about him.

"Are you seeing someone?"

"No. Why do you ask?"

"I don't know you seem to be a little distracted here and there and I see a different glow about you. Is this about that Julie woman that you saved?"

"I don't really feel comfortable talking to you about this."

"All right but she did something to you and I'm glad she came into your life. She's changed you and that's a good thing."

His boss left and he started to think some more. Maybe his boss was right he had changed since he started helping her and found out more information about her. The more he spent time with her the more he grew attached to her. It was really hard on him when she left to go back with David and then when he pushed her down the stairs and he sat with her in the hospital he knew that she needed him. She felt safe with him and he had protected her from him even if it was his own fault he even got to her in the first place. He should never have let his guard down. It almost cost Julie her life. He was glad that she had been smart about the dummy in bed. He heard the gunshots and thought that he had failed at protecting Julie and his heart sunk in chest. When he snuck up the stairs and heard her talking he knew that she was okay and he knew that she had seen him because she started to distract him so that he could sneak up on him. They were good together and those kisses what did that mean? He wasn't sure if it was because she was vulnerable and pregnant and she needed the kisses or if she had felt something between them. After analyzing everything he realized that he had fallen in love with Julie and it scared him to death. He had vowed to never love again but you can't plan on it when it falls in your lap. He still wasn't sure if she really felt the same for him or not. He was going to have to find out one way or another. He decided he was going to pay Sam a visit. He closed up his office and headed to the house. The closer he got the more nervous he got. He finally pulled up and was let in by the butler. Sam and Tony were at the kitchen table with Cole and Ashley but Julie wasn't there. Sam saw Mike and got up.

"What are you doing here?"

"I came to see you where is Julie?"

"She's sleeping. She hasn't been sleeping well Cole here doesn't like to sleep in the crib at night and she sleeps with him in the rocking chair. It's hard on her. I'm watching him while she catches up on some sleep."

"Don't you have to work soon?"

"Yeah but Tony said he would watch them both."

"I'll take Cole."

Sam handed Cole over to Mike and she smiled at him. She kissed Tony and left to go to work. Tony nodded at Mike and Mike went upstairs and saw that Julie was sleeping in her room. Mike saw that Cole was getting tired and put him down. He sat in the rocking chair watching him sleep. Like clockwork he was up in an hour and he was crying. Mike picked him up and held him and he stopped crying. He sat in the rocking chair and looked at Cole.

"Is this what you do to your mommy every night?"

Cole smiled and gurgled at him. Mike smiled at him.

"You should be nice to your mommy. She needs her sleep too. Why don't you and I just hang out for the night that way mommy can sleep tonight?"

Mike was still talking to him and singing him a lullaby until he fell asleep. He put Cole down to sleep and he was up in another hour. He didn't know that Julie had woken up and heard him talking to Cole. She smiled to herself and went back to sleep. She was really happy that Mike was there. It was the first night that she was able to sleep all the way through the night. She got up when the sun came pouring through the window and she didn't hear anything in the nursery. She got in the shower and put on a change of clothes and went into the nursery. She saw Mike sleeping with Cole in his arms. She smiled and carefully picked up Cole and took him down stairs to be fed. She was feeding Cole his bottle when Mike came down stairs. He saw that Julie was up and she looked like she had been refueled. While she was feeding him she was eating her own breakfast. She had really thinned out since Cole was born and she looked amazing. He was going to sneak out of the house before she saw him but he was close to the door when she grabbed his arm.

"Mike thank you for watching Cole last night. It was the first time I got any sleep through the night without him crying."

"It was no problem."

"Are you going to come back later?"

"I hadn't planned on it."

"I need to talk to you if you wouldn't mind coming back tonight when you get off work."

"I will try but I don't know what kind of case I'll be taking but I'll see what I can do."

Julie's smile faded and he left. He kicked himself on the way to work. Why did he do that to her? Julie deserved better than what he could give her anyway. He didn't want to get involved with her. He hadn't gotten any cases to work on so he left early. He was heading to Julie's and then decided against it. He went to his house and took a shower and then changed his clothes. He was watching television and was trying not to think about Julie but he couldn't help it. He finally got in his car and had decided to go over there. Sam and Tony were still up and Sam was on her way to work. She was heading out when Mike showed up at the door.

"I didn't think you were going to come by again."

"I hadn't planned on it but somehow I managed to drive here anyway."

"Well Julie is putting Cole down for his nap right now."

Mike went inside and headed up to the nursery. He stood off to the side so she couldn't see him. She was changing Cole and talking to him.

"Are you going to let me sleep tonight?"

Cole laughed at her and started to gurgle. She blew on his belly and he started laughing. She picked him up and swung him around a little bit and then she looked at him. Her smile had faded.

"I'm a horrible mother Cole. I can't even pick out a good daddy for you. I thought Mike would have wanted to be but I guess I was wrong about him too. Maybe it should just be you and me. We could get along without any one else right?"

Cole just gurgled more and she sat in the rocking chair with him.

"You don't care right now you are still too young to understand. The only thing David ever did right in our marriage is giving me you. I at least did something right in my life. It's a shame it wasn't the right way but at least I'll always have someone that loves me unconditionally. Are you ready to go to sleep or are you going to cry all night again?"

Cole just looked at her and she knew he had no clue what she was saying. She sang him a lullaby and he finally fell asleep. She put him down even though in an hour he would be up again. She covered him with the blanket and closed the door halfway when she saw Mike standing there.

"How long have you been out here?"

"Long enough."

"What are you doing here anyway? I thought you weren't going to stop by?"

"I changed my mind."

"Well you don't have to stay I don't want you to feel like I need you or anything. I'll let you get back to the life you had before I was in it."

Julie walked past Mike and went to her room. Mike

followed her and she was surprised that he was behind her when she went to close the door.

"Julie I'm sorry. I'm still not good with this relationship thing. I'm in love with you and I can't stop thinking about you. I do want to spend the rest of my life with you."

"You aren't saying that because you heard what I said to Cole are you?"

"No I've been so dumb and I can't get those kisses we had shared out of my head. I know that there was something between us but like you I wasn't sure if it was because of the situation or if it was because I was really in love with you. I don't want to lose you and Cole. I guess I finally realized that I can't help who I fall in love with."

Julie looked at him and she wasn't sure what to say. He moved closer to her and before she realized it he had kissed her. She didn't push him away this time and let him kiss her. They kissed for a little while and then she heard Cole crying. She left Mike and went to Cole. He was crying and she picked him up.

"Why now of all times. You better not be up all night tonight."

Cole had stopped crying and had fallen back to sleep and she put him down. She crept out of the room and ran into Mike.

"Are you sure you want to stick around? I mean he does that every hour on the hour. I don't get any peace."

"I want this and I want to be part of your family. I messed up with Sarah but I want to promise you this time I'm not going to mess up again. Julie will you marry me?"

Julie was shocked and saw the ring he was holding out

and she said yes with a tear rolling down her cheek and he put the ring on her finger. He picked her up and swung her around and they kissed. Things that were totally unexpected happened. Mike never thought he would love again but Julie had shown him that he could and even though Julie had a rough life she found the man she was meant to find. The unexpected wasn't a bad thing at all.

CPSIA information can be obtained at www.ICGtesting.com
Printed in the USA
LVOW082348020713

341138LV00001B/14/P